At the blast Ranson cried out and staggered. Colliding with the wall, he clutched his stomach. Blood pumped between his splayed fingers. He looked down, aghast, and said breathlessly, "No."

Fargo leveled the Colt. "I want a name."

Ranson oozed to the ground, his legs too weak to support him. "What?" he said, still staring at the wound and the blood.

"The name of whoever hired you and your pard, and why they want me dead."

"Bastard," Ranson said.

"The name or I'll shoot you again."

Ranson had dropped the Starr. He saw it and gritted his teeth and lunged.

Fargo kicked it away.

"Bastard, bastard, bastard," Ranson hissed. Shutting his eyes, he groaned.

"The name."

"Go to hell."

"You first." Fargo extended the Colt and thumbed back at the hammer. . . .

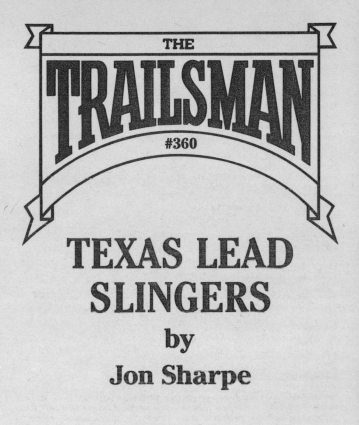

THE

TRAILSMAN

#360

TEXAS LEAD SLINGERS

by

Jon Sharpe

A SIGNET BOOK

SIGNET
Published by New American Library, a division of
Penguin Group (USA) Inc., 375 Hudson Street,
New York, New York 10014, USA
Penguin Group (Canada), 90 Eglinton Avenue East, Suite 700, Toronto,
Ontario M4P 2Y3, Canada (a division of Pearson Penguin Canada Inc.)
Penguin Books Ltd., 80 Strand, London WC2R 0RL, England
Penguin Ireland, 25 St. Stephen's Green, Dublin 2,
Ireland (a division of Penguin Books Ltd.)
Penguin Group (Australia), 250 Camberwell Road, Camberwell, Victoria 3124,
Australia (a division of Pearson Australia Group Pty. Ltd.)
Penguin Books India Pvt. Ltd., 11 Community Centre, Panchsheel Park,
New Delhi - 110 017, India
Penguin Group (NZ), 67 Apollo Drive, Rosedale, Auckland 0632,
New Zealand (a division of Pearson New Zealand Ltd.)
Penguin Books (South Africa) (Pty.) Ltd., 24 Sturdee Avenue,
Rosebank, Johannesburg 2196, South Africa

Penguin Books Ltd., Registered Offices:
80 Strand, London WC2R 0RL, England

First published by Signet, an imprint of New American Library,
a division of Penguin Group (USA) Inc.

First Printing, October 2011
10 9 8 7 6 5 4 3 2 1

The first chapter of this book previously appeared in *Platte River Gauntlet*, the three hundred fifty-ninth volume in this series.

The Trailsman

Beginnings . . . they bend the tree and they mark the man. Skye Fargo was born when he was eighteen. Terror was his midwife, vengeance his first cry. Killing spawned Skye Fargo, ruthless, cold-blooded murder. Out of the acrid smoke of gunpowder still hanging in the air, he rose, cried out a promise never forgotten.

The Trailsman they began to call him all across the West: searcher, scout, hunter, the man who could see where others only looked, his skills for hire but not his soul, the man who lived each day to the fullest, yet trailed each tomorrow. Skye Fargo, the Trailsman, the seeker who could take the wildness of a land and the wanting of a woman and make them his own.

The Gulf Coast of Texas, 1861—
where a high-stakes poker tournament
leads to deceit and death.

1

The two men latched on to Skye Fargo when he stopped at the saloon. He'd been on the trail for three days and wanted to wash the dust down before he went out to the mansion. Over a dozen of the top poker players in the country had been invited to take part in Senator Deerforth's annual high-stakes game, and he was on the list.

The sun had set and lights were coming on the length of Deerforth's main street. Named after the man who invited him, the Gulf town was booming. Silver was the reason; the largest deposit in south Texas.

The bar was three deep.

Fargo shouldered through and pounded on it to get the barkeep's attention. He hankered after a bottle but settled for a glass. Wiping his mouth with the sleeve of his buckskin shirt, he sauntered back out and was unwrapping the Ovaro's reins from the hitch rail when he became aware of a pair of hard-eyed men leaning against the wall. Their clothes marked them as sailors.

Fargo didn't think much of it and led the stallion down Main Street. When he glanced back the two men were following him. They tried not to be obvious but they might as well wear signs.

He didn't know what to make of it.

The next junction was Cutter Street. He turned right. Cutter ran down to the docks. A schooner was raising sail. Other ships were at anchor, some being loaded, others unloaded.

Fargo made for a broad patch of shadow cast by a clipper. A lantern glowed on board but no one was moving about. Letting the reins drop, he crouched and circled to a stack of crates.

The pair stopped about thirty feet away and gazed out to sea. The taller scratched under an arm and sniffed his fingers. The other fingered the hilt of a knife. They kept glancing at the Ovaro.

"What's he doing, Ranson?" asked the man with the knife. He had a chin that came to a point, and buckteeth.

"I can't tell much," the tall man replied. "I can see the horse but I can't see him."

"Do we do it or not?"

"We took half in advance, Jules."

"Then let's get it over with."

Ranson slid a dagger from his left sleeve. "We have to be careful. He's supposed to be tough."

"Tough, hell," Jules said. "You distract him and I'll earn us the rest."

"Nice of him to come to the docks," Ranson said. "Not many around at this time of day to notice."

"Damned nice," Jules agreed.

They moved toward the Ovaro.

By then Fargo had his Colt in his hand. He glided from behind the crates and smashed the barrel against Jules's head, pulping Jules's ear and felling him like a shot hog.

Ranson spun, his dagger glinting in the starlight. "What the hell," he blurted.

Fargo leveled his six-gun and thumbed back the hammer. "I wouldn't," he warned. "Not unless you want your brains splattered all over your pard."

Ranson straightened and dropped his dagger. "If this is a robbery we don't have much money, mister."

"Who paid you to kill me?"

"I don't know what in hell you're talking about," Ranson said.

"I heard you."

"You didn't hear us say nothing about killing. And since when is talk against the law, anyhow?"

"Do you see a badge?" Fargo said.

"If you were you might have some excuse for this but since you're not, you must be a footpad."

"The bluff won't wash."

"Then take us to the marshal and we'll see what he has to say."

Fargo had no proof the pair were plotting to assassinate him. It'd be their word against his.

"Well?" Ranson prodded.

Fargo could shoot them but one was unconscious and the other was unarmed.

"Are you going to stand there pointing that thing at me all night?"

"No," Fargo said, and slammed the Colt against Ranson's temple. The tall sailor joined his companion in a sprawled heap.

Twirling the Colt into his holster, Fargo climbed on the Ovaro. He hoped he wasn't making a mistake letting those two live.

Time would tell.

2

Senator Marion Deerforth was one of the richest men in the state, what with the family's shipping concerns and their plantation. He'd entered politics young and risen to prominence, and was well respected. His annual poker game brought in the cream of the professional fraternity.

Deerforth always reminded Fargo of a butterball. The man had three chins and folds of fat not even tailored suits could hide; he jiggled when he walked.

"Skye Fargo, as I live and breathe!" Deerforth exclaimed as he came down the marble steps. His hair was as white as snow, his face seamed with lines. "How are you doin', son?" he asked in his distinct drawl, and clapped Fargo on the arms. "I never know if you'll be able to make these poker shindys of mine."

"I try not to miss them," Fargo replied. They were more than poker games. It was a week of whiskey and women, and who could ask for more?

"You're the last to show," Senator Deerforth informed him. "Midnight is the deadline. You cut it close, as usual."

"I had a far piece to come," Fargo told him. Clear from the Green River country.

"Let's get you settled in and you can join me for drinks in my study."

"My horse—" Fargo said, and gestured at the Ovaro.

"My stable boys will take care of it as if it were my own." Deerforth gave him a jovial poke. "You should know that by now."

They were almost to the front door when a female version of Deerforth bustled out to greet them. She was just as wide and had just as many chins. "Skye!" she squealed in delight. "You handsome devil, you."

4

"Virginia," Fargo said.

"I prefer Ginny." She crushed him against her more-than-ample bosom. "How many times must I tell you that?"

"Now, now, my dear," the senator said. "Quit throwin' yourself at him."

"Be sensible," Ginny scolded. "He's young enough to be my son."

"Your grandson," Senator Deerforth said, and she playfully clipped him on the shoulder with her fist.

"True gentlemen never allude to a lady's age," Ginny scolded.

"Who says I'm a gentleman?"

"You'll be one in my presence, or else."

Fargo chuckled. They were always bickering, good-natured jibes that rolled off their backs like water off a duck. "Who showed up this year?"

"Lacey Mayhare," Ginny said, and winked. "She's been asking about you."

"Fine figure of a woman, that gal," Senator Deerforth said. "Were I single I'd show an interest."

"Show an interest and you will be," Ginny jousted. "Or dead, if I can find my derringer."

"Did you hear her?" Senator Deerforth said in mock dismay. "She wants my fortune for herself."

"Damn right I do," Ginny said, "and while I'm still young enough to enjoy spending it."

"Fifty-three isn't young, my dear."

"It sure as hell isn't old, either."

Fargo hoped he had half her spunk when he was her age. He'd rather not end his days in a rocking chair, twiddling his thumbs and counting the minutes until they planted him.

The parlor was as luxurious as Fargo remembered. A piano sat in a corner. The fireplace mantel was mahogany. Overhead, a chandelier sparkled. The people lounging and talking looked around as their hosts entered.

"Damn, not Fargo," said a handsome man in gambler garb. "I had my fingers crossed he wouldn't make it so I'd have a chance at winning." Smiling, he came over and offered his hand.

"Vin Creed, be nice to my other guests," Ginny chided.

"Fargo and I are well acquainted," Creed said as they shook. "If I have to lose to anyone, it might as well be him."

Beside Fargo a woman cleared her throat.

"It's a pleasure to see you again."

Fargo turned. Her voice was the sultriest in creation, a perfect fit for as fine a body as he'd ever come across.

From her golden hair to the tips of her small feet, she was exquisite. Her eyes were bluer than his, her lips as red as strawberries. "Lacey."

"Hard to believe a whole year has gone by."

At her touch a tingle shot up Fargo's arm. She always had that effect. Normally he wouldn't mind but her beauty distracted him from his card playing, and she knew it.

"I'm looking forward to taking more of your money."

Fargo winced. Last year he came to the tables with the entry fee of five thousand in his poke and left with forty-three dollars, mostly thanks to her. "You better not wear that perfume you did last time."

"You don't like ladies who smell nice?" Lacey rejoined, and laughed.

Senator Deerforth had his thumbs hooked in his vest and was rocking on his boot heels. "This year promises to be the best yet. We have twenty players, which brings the total pot to one hundred thousand dollars."

Vin Creed whistled. "I'd kill my own mother to win that much." He grinned at Fargo. "Or anyone else."

3

Another thing Fargo liked about his host was that Deerforth shared his fondness for liquor. The senator started each morning with whiskey in his coffee and the last thing he did before he went to bed each night was have a nightcap. It was rumored that Deerforth put down a bottle a day. Yet it never showed. Not once in the time Fargo had known him had he seen the senator drunk.

And now Deerforth ushered him to the liquor cabinet and said the words Fargo liked to hear.

"Help yourself, my friend."

Fargo was glad to. He opened a bottle of Monongahela, filled a large glass, and savored a sip. As the warmth spread through his gut he casually asked, "Do you happen to know anyone who'd want me dead?"

Deerforth studied him. "Are you implying someone tried to kill you?"

"They had it in mind," Fargo said, and briefly related his clash with Ranson and Jules.

"That's an outrage," the senator declared. "I'll fix their hash. I'll contact Marshal Moleen and have them arrested."

"For what? Waving knives around?"

"Damn it, man. You said that you heard them plotting to kill you."

"Can't arrest a man for talking." Fargo used Ranson's own argument.

"Why are you defending them? At least let me send Garvin and some men into town to find them and persuade them our climate isn't to their liking."

"Garvin" was the name of the hulking slab of muscle who ran the plantation. "No," Fargo said.

"Give me a reason."

"I'd like to find out who sicced them on me, and why."

"Garvin can find out."

"I stomp my own snakes," Fargo said, and treated himself to another swallow of liquid velvet.

"Suit yourself. But I think you're making a mistake."

"I do that a lot."

The senator put his hand on Fargo's shoulder. "I can't tell you how good it is to see you again, Skye. I get so tired of the silly bastards I have to put up with every day. The whiners and complainers and those with their hands out."

"You sound tired of it all."

"I am." Deerforth ran a hand over his white hair. "In case you haven't noticed, I'm getting on in years. I'm not going to run for reelection. I'm retiring at the end of this term."

"What will you do with yourself?"

"Drive poor Ginny crazy." Deerforth chuckled. "I don't know. Write my memoirs. Fish. Hunt. Drink a little."

"A little?"

They laughed, and the senator refilled his glass. "To old friends," he said, and started to raise it.

A girl swept into the room. Her black curls framed a round face that sparkled as bright as the chandelier. She wore a white cotton dress and white shoes. She went from guest to guest, smiling and friendly and bubbling with vitality.

"Ah, my sweet Roselyn," Deerforth said. "Our miracle baby, as Ginny likes to call her."

Fargo knew it had come as a surprise to the Deerforths to learn that Ginny was pregnant so late in life. That was fourteen years ago, and now the girl was the apple of their eye. They treated her like a princess yet she didn't act spoiled. Now she threw her arms around him and pressed her cheek to his chest.

"Uncle Skye!"

"We're not kin," Fargo always reminded her when she called him that.

Roselyn stepped back, grinning. "A good thing, too, or when I'm older it could cause a scandal."

"That's no way for a lady to talk," the senator said.

They hugged, the adoration in the father's eyes shining for all to see.

Fargo left them and mingled. He talked to a few players and came around a high-backed chair and there was Ginny with a glass in her lap. He was mildly surprised. She hardly ever touched the stuff. "What's the occasion, ma'am?"

"Old age."

"You don't look a day over forty."

Ginny's mouth crinkled. "Flatterer." She wagged the glass. "I'm getting into practice. Or haven't you heard that Marion is retiring?"

"I've heard."

"With him home all the time, I'll need it to steady my nerves."

"He's a lucky gent."

"No," Ginny said, "he's not." She drained half the glass without batting an eye or coughing.

"Damn, woman," Fargo said.

"It's not as if I never partake," Ginny confided. "I like a nip now and then."

"I'm shocked."

"We all have our secrets," Ginny said.

They happened to be near a window. About to take a swallow, Fargo glanced out of it and saw two men not twenty yards from the mansion.

It was Ranson and Jules.

4

In the time it took Fargo to reach the front door, the pair had vanished. He went down the steps three at a bound and paused at the bottom.

The plantation sprawled for hundreds of acres. Most of the land was devoted to cotton. Besides the mansion, there was a stable and more than a score of outbuildings.

The stable was lit as brightly as the house. Some of the guests were staying at the hotel in town, and carriages were lined up, the drivers waiting. A few had arrived on horseback and their animals were tied to a hitch rail.

Fargo went to the first carriage. The driver's arms were folded and his chin was on his chest; he appeared to be dozing.

"Did you see two men near here a minute ago?"

The man gave a start and looked up. "What? No, I didn't, mister."

The answer was the same at the next carriage and the one after that.

Fargo entered the stable. A black man was forking hay. No, no one had come in.

In a stall partway down stood the Ovaro. Fargo patted it and pondered and went out the back to the corral. Beyond were shacks, their windows aglow, and past them tilled fields.

Fargo saw no one and turned to go back. Out of the corner of his eye he caught movement. His hand on the Colt, he approached the corral. A dozen horses milled. A trough was near the gate. He started around it and a figure reared and was on him in the bat of an eye. He got his hand up as a knife speared at his chest and caught hold of a bony wrist. Fingers clamped onto his arm, preventing him from drawing the Colt.

"Got you now," Jules said, and kneed him.

Pain exploded in Fargo's groin. He tried to backpedal but Jules clung on. The man was strong, and determined. A foot hooked Fargo's ankle and the next he knew, he was on his back with Jules on his chest and the tip of the knife sinking toward his throat. He held it at bay but it took all his strength.

"Die, damn you."

Fargo was worried that Ranson would join in. He'd be easy to finish off, pinned as he was. To remedy that he bucked and rammed his head against Jules's chin. It was like ramming an anvil. His senses swam and he almost blacked out. He felt Jules wrench free and braced for the sting of the blade.

"What the hell is going on here?" a familiar voice demanded.

Suddenly the weight was off of Fargo's chest. He shook his head to clear it and saw Jules scrambling over the fence into the corral. Pushing to his knees, he palmed his Colt. Before he could fire, Jules was in among the horses. Fargo lost sight of him. Rising, he spotted a figure going over the rails on the far side. "Damn."

Vin Creed came up, a pearl-handled derringer in one hand, an unlit cigar in the other. "I repeat," he said. "What the hell was that about?"

"You tell me and we'll both know." Fargo shoved the Colt into his holster and turned. "He would have stabbed me if not for you. I'm obliged."

"What are friends for?" Creed's arm moved and the derringer disappeared up his sleeve.

Fargo had known the gambler for a few years now and considered him one of the best of the breed. But he still had to ask. "What are you doing out here?"

Creed raised the cigar. "I wanted a smoke and you know how fussy Ginny is."

Fargo grunted. He did indeed know that she couldn't abide the habit; cigar smoke made her ill. The senator had to smoke on their balcony or the porch.

"I came over to the stable and thought I heard someone out back," Creed went on. "Reckon I showed up at just the right time."

Fargo told him about the earlier attempt.

"Ranson and Jules, you say?" Creed scratched his chin. "I

11

seem to recollect hearing those names around. Hired muscle, you could call them. They beat up renters behind on their rent. That sort of thing. This is the first I've heard of them killing for pay."

"They're moving up in the world."

"Why murder you?"

"You tell me and we'll both know," Fargo said again. He was disgusted with himself at how Jules had almost gotten the better of him.

"You should tell Marion," Creed advised.

"Already did."

"He has no idea either?"

Fargo shook his head and rubbed his chest where Jules's knee had gouged him.

Creed proceeded to light his cigar. When the tip was glowing he let out a few puffs and remarked, "You know, it's not as if you haven't made a few enemies. Maybe one is trying to pay you back."

Fargo had thought of that. Most of his enemies, though, were dead. The few that weren't were either behind bars or far away. "I don't think it's someone I know."

"Then I reckon all you can do is wait for them to try again."

"That's the hell of it," Fargo said.

5

Fargo liked to stay at the mansion instead of the hotel. The hotel was close to the saloon where the game was held but the mansion had more to offer, not the least of which was a four-poster canopy bed. Lying on it was like sinking into a sea of feathers. He had removed his boots and gun belt and hat and plopped onto his back when someone knocked.

"You in there, good-looking?" Lacey Mayhare said.

Her tantalizing perfume wreathed him as Fargo opened the door. He admired the long sweep of her legs and how her lustrous golden hair cascaded over her shoulders. "To what do I owe the honor?"

"I'm not ready for bed yet." Lacey brushed past and moved to a chair. "I thought you might like some company."

Fargo shut the door and sat on the edge of the bed and regarded her suspiciously.

"What?"

"You're up to something."

"Me?" Lacey batted her eyes and laughter spilled from her smooth throat. "Whatever do you mean?"

"All you care about is winning," Fargo said. "You'll do anything to make sure you do."

"It's against Marion's rules to try to influence the outcome in any way," Lacey recited.

"That didn't stop you from trying to drink me under the table last year," Fargo reminded her. She'd almost done it, too. She was the only woman he'd ever met who could drink as much as he did and not pass out.

"Then I must have been trying to drink myself under the table, as well."

"And remember the year before that? You sent a bottle to

13

my room. I didn't drink it until after, which was lucky for me because it made me as sick as a dog."

"Coincidence," Lacey said. "There was a flu going around." She ran a hand down her leg and over her knee and smiled sweetly.

Fargo liked how her dress clung to her thighs. Tearing his gaze away, he said more gruffly than he intended, "Shouldn't you be getting back to the hotel?"

"Didn't you know? I'm staying with the Deerforths this year." Lacey shifted and somehow her bosom was twice the size it had been. "Ginny is such a dear. She invited me in past years but I always said no. This time I decided to take her up on it." Lacey bent toward him. "My room is right down the hall. Feel free to stop by any time of the day or night."

"No, you don't."

"Excuse me?"

"I'm here for the game," Fargo informed her, "and nothing else."

"What does that have to do with my invite?"

"I wasn't born yesterday." Fargo rose and went to the door. "Out you go."

"Honestly, now," Lacey said. "You're throwing me out on my ear?"

"On your ass," Fargo said, and opened the door.

"This won't change anything."

"Off you go."

Lacey rose and sashayed past and stopped in the doorway. "You'll regret this in the middle of the night when you want it and can't have it."

"Out."

Her dress swirled and she was gone but the scent of her perfume hung in the air.

Fargo closed the door and leaned against it. "What the hell did I just do?" He couldn't remember the last time he turned down a pretty woman, or any woman, for that matter. He started toward the bed and stopped at a loud knock. Thinking it was Lacey he jerked the door open, saying, "When I told you to go I—"

"What was that?" Ginny Deerforth said.

Fargo glanced right and left but saw no sign of Lacey. "What can I do for you, Virginia?"

"Marion just told me about that awful business at the corral. And that two men were out to do you harm in town."

"He should have kept it to himself."

"Don't be silly. We can't allow this. I had Marion send for Marshal Moleen. He should be here inside the hour."

Fargo sighed.

"Are you hurt?" Ginny asked, scrutinizing him from head to toes.

"Tired, is all," Fargo said. He'd had a long day in the saddle. "I'd like to get some sleep."

"After the marshal questions you, you can sleep all you want." Ginny patted his arm. "I'm sorry about this. So very sorry."

"It's not as if you had anything to do with it."

"I know. But to have a guest assaulted at our home. It's unthinkable." Ginny wrung her hands. "I apologize for being so flustered. I don't like violence. It sickens me."

"Sometimes a person doesn't have a choice."

"I know that. I'm not naïve. Texas was born in violence. The war with Mexico, the Alamo, San Jacinto. Violence has held the Comanches in check. Violence keeps the outlaws in line." Ginny did more hand-wringing. "Yes, there are times when it's called for. I just wish that wasn't the case."

Fargo smiled, thinking she would go, but she wasn't done.

"Should whoever is out to kill you succeed, rest assured I'll personally see to it that you're buried proper, with a headstone and everything."

"How sweet of you," Fargo said.

6

The Cosmopolitan was the fanciest saloon in town. The senator owned it. The tables were covered in green velvet. Behind the mahogany bar was the largest selection of liquor west of the Mississippi. The bartenders wore aprons.

The annual poker event brought booming business. Folks came from all over Texas and parts beyond.

Politicians never let a crowd go to waste and the senator was no exception. He always gave a speech at the start of the festivities.

By Fargo's reckoning about two hundred people were out in the street listening. He was fond of the man but he'd be damned if he'd listen to him prattle so he sat in the saloon sipping whiskey and riffling cards.

"Mind if I join you?" Vin Creed asked, and sank down across from him. Creed wore a frock coat and a wide-brimmed black hat. "Ready to lose all your money to me?"

"That'll be the day," Fargo said.

The same perfume as the night before tingled Fargo's nose, and Lacey Mayhare came around from behind him and claimed another chair. Today she had on a black dress, her breasts practically bursting from the seams. Her lips were ruby red. "If anyone takes Skye's poke," she said to the gambler, "it'll be me."

"Morning, my dear," Creed said. "Up to your usual tricks, I see."

"Tricks?" Lacey said.

"That pair of watermelons you call tits," Creed said. "I'm surprised you don't let the nipples show."

Where many women would have been offended, Lacey

merely smiled. "Are you suggesting that I wear this low-cut dress on purpose?"

"I am."

"And that I use my watermelons, as you so quaintly call them, to take my opponents' minds off their cards so they play poorly?"

"You do."

"Why, sir," Lacey said, and beamed, "you are exactly right. And do you know something?"

"I know many things," Creed said. "To which do you refer?"

"If you had melons, you'd do the same as me."

"Perhaps," the gambler said. "Although I'd like to think I have more dignity."

"Excuse me?"

"I rely on skill, my dear. I am, as our mutual friend here will confirm"—Creed nodded at Fargo—"an honest gambler."

"There's no such animal," Lacey declared. "You've never dealt from the bottom of the deck? Never shaved a card?"

"I don't need to."

Lacey switched her attention to Fargo. "Do you believe him?"

"Just because you cheat," Fargo said, "doesn't mean everybody does."

Her eyes flashed with anger but it quickly faded. "Perhaps, and I stress *perhaps*, normally I am not above shading luck in my favor. But not here. Here I play as honest a game as Mr. Creed pretends to."

"You don't have a choice," Fargo said. "Deerforth throws out anyone who cheats."

"And they're never allowed to take part in another of his tournaments," Creed said.

"These are grand, aren't they?" Lacey said, gazing about. "There isn't a finer saloon anywhere." She sobered and stared at Fargo. "What's this I hear about someone trying to kill you?"

"Hell," Fargo said.

"Ginny told me this morning. She's worried about you, the sweet dear."

"Ginny is a busybody."

"Now, now. You should be flattered she cares." Lacey indicated a man over at the bar. "You have her to thank for him."

"What are you talking about?"

"Ginny demanded that Marshal Moleen assign a man to watch over you. Deputy Gilmore, there, is your protector."

"Damn."

"I wish I had a protector," Creed said.

Fargo glared.

"Look at the bright side," Lacey said. "With Gilmore watching your back, you can concentrate on your cards."

Fargo wasn't about to trust his life to a man he didn't know. He let it drop, though. He wouldn't play well if he was angry. And suddenly it hit him. "Bitch," he said.

Lacey batted her eyes. "What did I do?"

"You knew how I'd feel about Ginny and the marshal," Fargo said.

"Isn't she wonderful?" Creed said. "There's no end to her tricks."

Lacey smiled and ran a hand down her neck and over her bosom. "Why, gentlemen, whatever do you mean?"

7

The speech ended and Senator Deerforth led a procession
into the saloon. The mayor, the members of the town council
and Marshal Moleen were followed by some of the top poker
players in the country; Dandy Dan from Saint Louis, Aces
O'Bannon from New Orleans, Sly Jackson, known as the
King of the Mississippi Riverboats, and others.

As the spectators gawked, one by one the gamblers filed
past Senator Deerforth and handed over the five thousand-
dollar entry fee. The mayor then gave them their chips.

Fargo's turn came. He dropped his poke into the senator's
palm and Deerforth turned and added it to the collection of
pokes and wallets and purses in a great silver bowl. "Don't
lose it," he joked.

"Never fear," Deerforth said jovially, and bobbed his chins
at Moleen. "Our good marshal will personally escort the
bowl to the bank where it will be deposited in the safe until
the winner is decided."

Lacey was next, a leather bag with a strap dangling from
her fingers. "Here you are, Marion. I'll expect it back when I
pick up my winnings."

"Confidence becomes you, my dear."

"Everything becomes me," Lacey said.

"Especially those tits of yours," Vin Creed said as he
tossed his poke to the senator.

Five tables in the middle of the room were reserved for
the tournament. Four chairs ringed each table, and on the
back of each was a sign with a number. From a hat, the players drew slips of paper with corresponding numbers.

Fargo drew chair nineteen. He found himself at a table
with Aces O'Bannon and two gamblers he didn't know.

Sealed decks were placed on the tables.

"Ladies and gentlemen," Senator Deerforth grandly announced, "let the games begin."

Onlookers were not allowed within six feet of the tables. The crowds were well behaved. Anyone who caused a ruckus or interfered with the players in any way was summarily, and often roughly, ejected.

Fargo got down to the business of playing poker and shut out everything else. His first hand wasn't promising. He ended up with a pair of twos. The next hand he had nothing. And the one after that. He was beginning to think it was an omen when he was dealt three kings and two tens. After that, his luck changed.

By six that evening only Aces O'Bannon was left. Aces had more chips and he was growing cocky. The next hand he bet heavy on two pair and lost to Fargo's three of a kind.

"You're a devil with the cards and that's for sure," O'Bannon complimented him.

"I've had a lot of practice," Fargo said. He wet his throat with whiskey but only a swallow. He'd been nursing a glass all afternoon.

O'Bannon gazed about them. "'Tis a fine affair, this tournament of the senator's, is it not?"

Fargo wasn't in the mood for talk. All he did was grunt.

"Come visit New Orleans sometime and I'll treat you to a night you won't soon forget."

"I've been there."

"Then you know the charms of the Creole girls. I can introduce you to one who will make you forever glad you're a man, if you get my drift."

"O'Bannon?"

"Yes, laddie?"

"Shut the hell up."

O'Bannon colored and gripped the edge of the table. "I was only being friendly."

"Play cards," Fargo said.

It was O'Bannon's turn to deal. He did so with fluid ease, the cards an extension of his fingers.

Fargo detected no evidence of cheating. He had a pair of fours, a seven, a jack and a king. He asked for three cards and was glad he had a poker face—he wound up with two more fours.

O'Bannon toyed with his chips, stacking and restacking them. Finally he said, "I have to go with my gut and my gut says I've got you beat. How much do you have there?"

Fargo told him.

O'Bannon counted out the amount and pushed the pile to the center.

Fargo didn't hesitate. "All in," he said, adding his chips to the pile.

"A flush," O'Bannon declared, showing his hand. He was so confident he reached for the pot.

"Not so fast," Fargo said. "You must have indigestion." He turned his cards over.

O'Bannon swore. From then on he played recklessly, seeking to recoup his winnings. He lost that much faster.

A straight sealed O'Bannon's fate. He shook hands and made for the bar.

Fargo had twenty thousand in chips. It wasn't the most he'd ever won but it was close. Unfortunately, the rules didn't let players cash out early. It was winner take all. He had to see it through to the end.

Five other players had been eliminated. He could claim any of the seats and continue. Trying to decide, he glanced from table to table.

Lacey caught his eye. She grinned and blew him a kiss.

8

Fargo joined her table. Inside of two hours only she and he were left. They battled back and forth and neither gained an advantage. At midnight Senator Deerforth announced that the first day of the tournament was officially concluded and they would resume the next morning at nine.

Fargo rubbed his eyes and leaned back and stretched. Lacey was regarding him with an amused expression. She hadn't said much while they played. She was always serious about her cards.

"Tired, handsome?"

"Not really," Fargo said. He'd taken part in games that lasted two days or better.

"Me either. How about you be a gentleman and treat me to a meal?"

There was only one restaurant in town and during the tournament it stayed open twenty-four hours. Fargo ordered beef and potatoes. Lacey preferred eggs and bacon.

"So have you figured out who's trying to kill you yet?" she asked out of the blue while they were waiting for their food.

Fargo shook his head.

"It isn't me," Lacey said, and laughed.

"I'm glad you find it so funny."

"Oh, I don't. Believe me. I like you, Skye. You try so hard to resist my charms. *That's* funny."

"Why?"

"You, of all people."

"You're used to men falling all over you."

Lacey sat back, her eyes crinkling. "It's not that. It's you. Skye Fargo. The great lover. You have a reputation, you know.

Let me see. How does it go?" She tapped her chin and pretended to be trying to remember. "Ah, yes. You've never met a female you haven't bedded."

"There have been a few," Fargo allowed.

"There have been a hell of a lot more than that. I bet you can't remember them all. I bet you've lost count."

"Why are we talking about this?"

"Because I'm trying to spark interest."

"In what."

"Me."

Fargo stared.

"I was thinking that you and I could go back to my room and spend the night together."

"Just like that? You come right out with it?"

"Why not?" Lacey said. "Does it always have to be the man who makes the first move?"

"True love, huh?"

"Damn you," Lacey said, but she was smiling. "I need rest. I need to sleep so I'll be fresh for the tournament tomorrow. And the best way I know to relax and drift off is to go to bed with someone."

"You just happened to pick me?"

"God, you have a suspicious mind."

"I know you, Lacey. What was it Vin said? There's no end to your tricks."

"This isn't a trick. All I want to do is fuck you."

The waitress brought their plates. Fargo was famished and dug right in. He didn't pay attention to his companion until she cleared her throat.

"Well?"

"Well what?"

"Don't play games. Have you made up your mind? Is it yes or is it no?"

"I'm still thinking." Fargo forked a thick piece of meat rimmed with fat into his mouth and chewed with relish.

"Most men would leap at the chance."

"Most men don't know you like I do."

Lacey delicately broke off a small piece of scrambled egg and speared it and placed it in her mouth.

Fargo tried not to think of her breasts and how it would be to have his hands on them. He ate some more and washed it down with a mouthful of coffee.

"I've always liked you," Lacey said.

"Stop it."

"Can't we call a truce? Our lovemaking would have nothing to do with the cards. In the morning we'll go our separate ways and your life will go on as usual."

Fargo tried to recollect the last time a woman had to talk him into climbing under the sheets with her, and couldn't.

"What are you grinning about?"

"How damn silly life can be."

"You think I'm silly for wanting to go to bed with you?"

"I think you're as good-looking a woman as I've ever come across but I don't trust you any further than I can throw a buffalo."

Lacey's luscious lips curled. "A compliment at last."

"You're forgetting the trust part."

"I give you my solemn word that this isn't a trick. What more can I say?"

Fargo looked at her breasts and at her mouth and at her hair and heard himself say, "We go to my room, not yours."

"Deal," Lacey said.

9

It was that damn perfume of hers. It got into a man's head and wouldn't let go.

Lacey sashayed past and over to the bed and tossed her bag on the dresser. She put her hands on her hips and arched her back and her breasts pushed against her dress. "Like what you see?"

Fargo shut the door. The mansion was quiet. Everyone else was already in bed.

"Cat got your tongue?"

Unbuckling his gun belt, Fargo placed it beside her bag. He walked over and stood in front of her but didn't touch her.

"What are you waiting for?" she impatiently asked.

"Hell to freeze over."

Lacey tapped her foot and frowned. "If you've changed your mind, say so. I'll go to my own room."

Fargo called her bluff. He stepped aside and motioned at the door. "See you in the morning."

A red tinge spread from Lacey's neck line to her hair. "You son of a bitch."

Fargo stood there. She glared and stamped her foot and then she stared and when he didn't say anything, she snorted and laughed.

"You're playing with me, aren't you?"

Fargo cupped her breasts and squeezed. Lacey gasped and stiffened. He squeezed harder and her eyelids fluttered. Suddenly she was pressed against him, her mouth hungrily glued to his, panting in her need. Her fingers found his hair and his hat fell to the floor.

Sliding his hands under her backside, Fargo lifted her and

swept her onto the four-poster bed. He set her on her back and took off his spurs.

Lacey scooted up so her head was on the pillow. Her beautiful features framed by a golden halo of hair, she crooked a leg and languidly moved it back and forth. She crooked a finger, too, and touched the nail to her red lips. "Now this is more like it," she said huskily.

Fargo stretched out beside her. He ran a hand from her neck to her waist and she mewed. When he kissed her, her mouth was molten. Her tongue darted and probed. He sucked on it and she sucked on his. He began to undo a row of tiny buttons that ran down the middle of her back. It took a while. There were dozens.

Fargo kissed her neck, her ear. He nipped a lobe. He ran his other hand through her hair and was pricked by a silver hairpin he'd noticed earlier. Without thinking about it, he plucked the hairpin out and let it fall.

For her part, Lacey's hands were everywhere. She pulled at his buckskin shirt and slid a hand underneath. Her fingers roved over his washboard gut and up his broad chest.

At last Fargo got the dress down around her waist. He eased her chemise off one shoulder and low enough to expose a breast. Her nipple popped free and he devoured it. He swirled it with his tongue and lightly bit it and she ground against him and cooed.

Lacey bit him. She bit his ear and his neck and she sank her teeth into his shoulder.

Fargo grew warm all over. Below his belt a bulge swelled. When Lacey brazenly placed a hand on his pole, it throbbed. Baring her other breast, he lavished his tongue on both. She tasted of powder and perfume.

Rising onto his knees, Fargo peeled off her dress and then the chemise. She had on stockings but he left those on. Her shoes joined his spurs on the floor.

Lacey returned the favor. She pulled off his shirt and threw it down and eagerly slid his pants around his shins. She couldn't get them any lower because of his boots. As his member came free she gasped.

"Good Lord. I had no idea."

She fondled him and cupped him, and Fargo's throat constricted. He pressed his lips to her shoulder, to her melons, to her flat belly. She pressed hers to his neck and shoulders.

Abruptly dipping, Lacey looked up at him and grinned, then applied her mouth.

Now it was Fargo who gasped. He closed his eyes and tilted his head back and let the exquisite sensation wash over him. She knew just what to do. It took every ounce of self-control he possessed not to explode. After she had been at it a while, he pulled her up and kissed her and dropped his hand to the junction of her thighs. He ran a finger along her slit. She was wet and ready. He touched her tiny knob and she shivered. He rubbed, and she thrust her hips at his.

Fargo inserted a finger. He inserted another. She held herself still and scarcely seemed to breathe. When he stroked, her bottom came up off the bed and she smothered an outcry. Her fingers enfolded him and her hand mimicked the rhythm of his. Their mouths were twin volcanoes.

A considerable while passed before Fargo eased between her legs. She hooked her ankles behind him and looked into his yes.

"Yes. Do me."

Fargo ran the tip of his manhood up and down, wetting it. With a flip of her hip she sought to impale him but he pulled back.

"Quit playing games, damn it," Lacey said.

"I aim to please, ma'am," Fargo replied, and drove up into her to the hilt.

Lacey's eyes widened and her mouth parted and her back bent into a bow.

"How was that?" Fargo said, holding himself still.

Lacey moaned.

"There's more yet," Fargo told her, and settled into a rocking motion. The velvet feel of her inner walls brought him to the brink but he held off. Under them the bed tossed as if on a storm-swept sea. Above them the canopy shook. Again and again he rammed into her. She clamped her legs and their two bodies became a single machine, thrusting and counterthrusting, their passion rising until they were poised at the cusp.

"Now," Lacey pleaded. "Please."

"Ladies first," Fargo said, and reaching between them, he touched a finger to her.

Lacey gushed. She churned. She dug her teeth and her nails into him. She pushed her face into a pillow to muffle her moans.

Fargo let himself go. When he eventually came to a stop and collapsed on top of her, he was caked with sweat. Rolling off her, he lay on his side.

"That was nice," Lacey said dreamily, her eyes half-shut, a finger playing with her hair.

Fargo grunted.

"We should have done it years ago."

Closing his eyes, Fargo was content to drift off. The long day and the full meal had caught up to him. Just as he was about to slip under, she jabbed his jaw with a fingernail.

"You're not going to sleep on me, are you?"

"I was thinking about it," Fargo said.

"I can't say much for your stamina."

Fargo looked at her.

"Well, I can't."

"What are you up to?"

"Nothing. I'd just like a second helping. We don't have to be at the saloon until nine and I'm not tired yet."

"I am." Fargo turned his back to her and nestled his chin on a pillow. He half expected her to argue but she didn't and soon he slipped into dreamland. He slept soundly, much more so than usual, so soundly that he didn't wake up at the crack of day as he usually did.

Sunlight was streaming in the window when Fargo finally opened his eyes. He felt sluggish and couldn't quite focus. He went to sit up and heard a peculiar sound and discovered his right arm wouldn't move.

He was handcuffed to the bedpost.

10

Suddenly Fargo was wide awake. He swore and tugged and hurt his wrist. Turning, he saw an impression on the quilt where Lacey had been lying.

Fargo opened his mouth to shout but didn't. He'd look the fool. Once word spread he'd be a laughingstock. After venting his spleen with a string of curses, he took a few deep breaths to calm himself and bent over the cuffs. Clearly stamped on both bracelets was the word WILSON, they were manufactured by the T. H. Wilson company. He was familiar with them. Law officers used Wilson cuffs a lot. It took a special key with a round stem to unlock them.

Fargo rested his chin on his arm and pondered. Why Lacey had done it was obvious. The rules stated that the tournament started at nine sharp. Anyone who didn't show up was disqualified. There were no exceptions.

The angle of the sunlight streaming in the window suggested it was past seven, probably later. He had to undo the cuffs and get to the saloon and he didn't have a lot of time.

The cuff fit so tight around his wrist that slipping his hand through was out of the question. He'd need grease or oil to make it slippery enough, and even then he'd lose a lot of skin and some flesh besides.

The post was too thick to break. He could kick it for half the day and it would hold up.

No, Fargo decided, he had to undo the cuffs. But how, when he didn't have the damn key? An idea occurred to him. Shifting, he hiked at his right pant leg and slid his left hand into his boot and palmed his Arkansas toothpick.

Toothpicks were different from most knives in that most

had a single sharp edge but toothpicks were double-edged and came to a fine point.

Fargo inserted the tip into the keyhole. It went in a quarter of an inch and he felt it press against the mechanism.

He pushed but nothing happened. He twisted to the right with the same result. He twisted to the left and thought he could feel something give but the cuff didn't come unfastened.

Fargo did more swearing. He sat back and noticed a gleam on the quilt where Lacey's head had been; it was the silver hairpin.

Fargo slid the Arkansas toothpick into its ankle sheath and snatched up the hairpin. A lot of women used them but not many could afford hairpins made of sterling silver. He slid it into the keyhole on the cuff and moved it from side to side and twisted one way and then the other. Once again nothing happened. He slid it a fraction farther and turned it as he would a key and there was a slight click. Elated, he pulled on the cuff but it stayed fastened.

Fargo slumped on the pillow. He didn't know how much time he had but it couldn't be a lot. He had to get the cuff off and get to the Cosmopolitan or he'd forfeit his five thousand dollars and any chance of winning. His temper flared, and in a burst of anger he stuck the hairpin into the hole and pushed harder and twisted almost savagely.

There was a louder click and the cuff popped open.

Quickly, Fargo found his shirt and was soon dressed with his gun belt around his waist. He opened his door and ran to the stairs. Someone was in the parlor, humming. He was more interested in the grandfather clock in the hall. "Seventy thirty-seven," he said out loud, relieved. He'd thought it was a lot later.

"Who's there?" a female voice said, and out of the parlor came young Roselyn Deerforth, as cute as could be in a pink dress with a matching pink bow in her hair. "Oh. Mr. Fargo. Are you feeling better?"

"How's that again?" Fargo said.

Roselyn smiled sweetly. "Miss Mayhare told my parents and me that you were feeling poorly."

"She did, did she?"

Roselyn nodded. "She said you had too much to drink last night and it made you sick." Roselyn pointed her left forefinger at him and ran her right forefinger along the top of it. "Shame on you."

"The bitch," Fargo said.

"Mr. Fargo!" Roselyn put a hand to her throat and took a step back.

"What else did she say?"

Roselyn looked scared. "Only that we weren't to disturb you no matter what. My father wanted to go up but Miss Mayhare said you were passed out in a stupor. That was her very word. Stupor."

"Is the senator here?"

"No, he left for his saloon a while ago. Mother is, though. She's in the kitchen with Garvin. Want me to take you to her?"

"No, thanks." Fargo touched his hat brim and hurried outdoors. The bright glare made him squint. He crossed to the stable and went down the aisle to the Ovaro's stall. Opening it, he slipped on the bridle and brought the stallion out. He threw on the saddle blanket, smoothed it, and grabbed hold of the saddle. As he was about to swing it up and over, the Ovaro nickered and feet slapped the ground behind him. He turned just as the man called Jules sprang at him with a knife raised to stab him in the back.

11

Fargo jerked the saddle up and the blade bit into the cantle. He shoved the saddle at Jules, let it fall, and swooped his hand to his Colt. Before he could draw, arms wrapped around him from behind. Instinctively, he drove his head back and smashed it into the face of his second attacker. The man cursed and the arms slackened. Fargo glanced down, saw a boot, and brought his heel down on it while thrusting his elbow back as hard as he could. The next instant he was free.

The second man was Ranson. Blood smeared his nose. Reaching behind him, he produced a knife.

Jules was in a crouch, poised to pounce.

At the front of the stable someone screamed. Roselyn, with her face twisted in horror.

Ranson and Jules glanced at her and Ranson said a strange thing. "Not now." With that they bolted for the rear of the stable.

Fargo would be damned if he'd let them get away again, and started after them.

"Skye! Wait!" Roselyn yelled.

Fargo stopped.

Ranson made it through the back door, Jules a step behind him.

Fargo raised the Colt. He could easily put a slug into the man's back. Instead, he snapped the Colt down and said, "Damn me all to hell." Wheeling, he shoved the Colt into his holster.

Roselyn was running down the aisle. "Are you all right? Did they hurt you?"

"Was that all you wanted?"

His gruff tone stopped her in her tracks. "I was afraid for you. I thought they were going to kill you."

"They keep trying," Fargo said. "What are you doing out here, anyway?"

"I came out to tell you that you better hurry into town," Roselyn said. "I forgot to mention that Miss Mayhare was trying to get Father to start the tournament early today."

"What?"

"You should have seen her," Roselyn related. "She was touching him and rubbing against him and Mother didn't like it one bit."

Fargo made himself a promise, then and there. "Let's get you inside."

Just then a man as tall as a redwood and as wide as a wall entered the stable. He wore a brown hat and a brown vest and work clothes, but no revolver. His square face was framed by spikes of dark hair. "What's going on in here? What was that scream about?"

"Garvin!" Roselyn exclaimed. "Some men were trying to hurt Skye."

Garvin Oster lumbered toward them. "Fargo," he said curtly by way of greeting. "The senator told me what happened out at the corral. He asked me to keep an eye on things."

"You're doing a good job," Fargo said.

"Hey, now." Garvin balled his huge fists. "I don't like your tone."

"Watch her," Fargo said, with a nod at the girl. He figured it was pointless but he ran to the rear door. Ranson and Jules were nowhere to be seen. Simmering, he returned to the Ovaro and picked up his saddle.

Garvin Oster and Roselyn hadn't moved.

"What do you reckon it's all about?" the foreman asked.

"Find those two bastards and I'll find out." Fargo swung the saddle on and bent to the cinch.

"You shouldn't cuss in front of Roselyn," Garvin told him.

"It's all right," Roselyn said.

"No, it's not." Garvin gently placed a hand on her arm. "You're almost a grown lady. Anyone doesn't treat you right, I'll break them in half." He looked meaningfully at Fargo.

"My father swears now and then," Roselyn said.

"He shouldn't."

"Oh hell," Fargo said. He was finished with the saddle

33

and stepped into the stirrups. "You might want to get her inside and search the plantation for those two sailors."

"How do you know that's what they do?"

"Their clothes, their caps," Fargo said. "They sure as hell aren't farmers."

"There you go swearing again."

"Give my regards to your mother," Fargo said to Roselyn, and tapped his spurs. He trotted out of the stable and brought the Ovaro to a gallop.

The air helped clear his head. By the time he reached town and drew rein at a hitch rail, he had his temper under control.

Or thought he did until he barreled into the Cosmopolitan, and there was Lacey Mayhare.

12

Senator Deerforth and Lacey were talking and laughing over by the bar. The senator was saying something in her ear when Fargo walked up, unnoticed, and motioned for the bartender to bring him a drink. As soon as he had the glass in his hand, he stepped over to them.

"Remember me?"

Lacey started and turned. "Skye!" she exclaimed, as if she was happy to see him. "This is a delightful surprise."

"I'll bet," Fargo said, and upended the glass over her head. Shock riveted her and everyone who had seen it.

"What on earth?" Senator Deerforth blurted. "What's gotten into you?"

Fargo smacked the glass on the bar. "The next time you handcuff a man to a bed, don't leave this lying around." He fished the silver hairpin from his pocket and smacked it down next to the glass.

Lacey sputtered and dabbed at the whiskey running down her face and neck. "You—you—you—" She couldn't seem to find a word fitting enough.

"What was that about handcuffs?" Senator Deerforth asked.

"She tried to make me late so I'd miss the tournament," Fargo enlightened him.

"Oh, Lacey," Deerforth said.

"I did no such thing!" she snapped, and spit out whiskey that had trickled into her mouth.

"You claim he's lying?" the senator said.

"What proof does he have?" Lacey accepted a towel the bartender offered.

"I have to tell you," Senator Deerforth said, "that I've known this man a good number of years now, and I've never heard him tell a falsehood. He has his faults but lying isn't one of them."

"What faults?" Fargo said.

"It's his word against mine," Lacey told Deerforth, "and I say I didn't do it."

"Are you behind those two men trying to kill me, too?"

"I don't know what in God's name you're talking about, you big lummox."

"You want to win more than anything," Fargo said. "You told me so, yourself."

"I'd never resort to *murder*."

"I wouldn't put anything past you," said someone else, and out of the crowd strolled Vin Creed, a deck of cards in his hand. "Fargo's right, my dear. You'd drown your own mother to win a hundred thousand dollars."

"Go to hell," Lacey rejoined.

The gambler laughed. "I have no doubt I will. And when you show up, I'll have a table reserved."

Lacey glared at them and at the senator and marched toward the back, pushing and shoving anyone not quick enough to get out of her way.

"Isn't she beautiful?" Creed said.

"I'll have to disqualify her," Senator Deerforth said. "The rules are clear. Participants aren't permitted to interfere with other players in any way."

"No," Fargo said.

"I beg your pardon?"

"Don't kick her out of the tournament."

"She cheated."

"There's a shock," Vin Creed said.

The senator glanced at him in annoyance and turned back to Fargo. "She cheated yet you want her to stay in? What am I missing?"

"It must be love," Creed said.

"Don't you have something to do?" Deerforth asked in exasperation.

"No."

"Well, go do something anyway." To Fargo the senator said, "I'm waiting for an explanation."

"I'd rather beat her fair."

"It *is* love," Creed said.

Deerforth drummed his fingers on the bar. "Are you drunk, Mr. Creed?"

"I wish to hell I was," Creed said wistfully. "But I never drink on days I play cards."

"That's quite commendable."

"Commendable, hell. I play piss-poor when I drink and I can't afford to lose."

Senator Deerforth turned back to Fargo. "Where were we?"

"You were going to ask to be best man at his wedding," Creed said.

"I give up," Deerforth declared.

"Lacey stays in?" Fargo wanted to know.

"If that is your wish, yes. However, any more shenanigans on her part and out she goes." Deerforth stared at Creed. "Now if you'll excuse me, for some reason I feel like I need a drink."

"Does Mrs. Deerforth know you're a lush?" Creed asked.

The senator went, "Harrumph," or made a sound to that effect, and stalked off muttering.

"Some folks have no sense of humor," Vin Creed said.

13

Fargo's day had started lousy and it got worse. An hour into day two of the tournament he was down half his stake. He bet heavy on three kings and lost and bet heavier on a flush and lost again.

Dandy Dan from Saint Louis was across from him. On his right was a timid player who nearly always folded at the first cards dealt and on his left a man who was much too reckless.

Fargo concentrated on Dandy Dan. Dan was a professional, a veteran with thirty years at the tables. His face was a blank slate and he bet with a casual detachment that made him impossible to read.

The reckless player was the first to lose his chips. He went all in on a straight. Unfortunately for him, Dandy Dan had a full house.

The timid player clung on. Now and then he'd open but he always buckled if they raised.

Fargo had an idea but he had to wait almost an hour for the cards to fall his way. He was dealt a pair of aces. The timid player opened and Fargo stayed in but didn't raise. Fargo asked for three cards and got another ace. The timid player raised.

Fargo pretended to mull it over and after a long interval he announced, "I'm going all in."

The timid player gulped. He looked at his cards and at the pile and at his cards again and he forced a nonchalant grin and said, "I'll call."

It turned out he had two pair, queens and jacks.

"Nicely done," Dandy Dan said as Fargo raked in his winnings. "Now it's just the two of us."

"And in a while it will just be me."

Dandy Dan smiled. "I admire a man with confidence, even when it's misplaced."

For the next three hours the advantage seesawed back and forth. One or the other would get ahead only to lose most of what he had gained.

Dandy Dan mentioned he was thirsty and signaled the bartender, who brought a pitcher of water and a glass. "Care to partake?"

"Why not?" Fargo said.

"Another glass, if you please." Dan filled the first glass and slid it over. "Be my guest."

Fargo wet his throat and set the glass back down. "You're a long way from Saint Louis," he said by way of small talk.

"For a hundred thousand dollars I'd travel to China and back." Dandy Dan smoothed his sleeve. "I win this, it's my last hurrah. I'll have all I need to spend the rest of my days in comfort."

"You're getting out?"

"You see these gray hairs? I'm not the player I used to be."

"Couldn't prove that by me."

Dandy Dan was smoothing his other sleeve, and stopped. "What a damn fine thing to say. I mean that. You're good, too. Damn good, or I'd have cleaned you out by now."

The bartender brought the other glass.

"There's a rumor going around that two men tried to kill you," Dandy Dan said as he poured. "Is that true?"

Fargo nodded. "Fortunately they are piss-poor at it."

"Is one of them short and stocky and looks as if he should be mopping the deck on a ship?"

"How in hell would you know that?"

"He walks past the front window once an hour or so and peers in at you," Dandy Dan said.

Fargo glanced at the glass plate that filled half the front wall.

"How is it you noticed him?"

"I'm a gambler," Dandy Dan said, as if that explained everything.

"I gamble too."

"But not for a living, I understand. There's a difference."

"Cards are cards," Fargo said.

39

The professional from Saint Louis smiled. "That's where you're mistaken. I've watched you play. You read the other players well. But that's as far as you take it."

Fargo was curious. "What more is there?"

"A gambler worthy of the name doesn't just read the players," Dandy Dan said. "He reads the table, he reads the room, he reads everything and everyone around him. I can tell you how many people have come and gone since the games started. I can tell you how much our opponents bet on every hand. I can tell you that the man who stares in at you has brown eyes and is bald around the ears and has a knife on his left hip."

"Damn," Fargo said.

"I can tell you something else," Dandy Dan said. "I've seen that man before. Several days ago, in fact, when I arrived in town."

"You did?"

"Yes," Dandy Dan said. "When I saw him he was talking to an acquaintance of yours."

Fargo tingled with expectation. "Who?"

"Lacey Mayhare."

14

It nearly cost Fargo the game. He became so caught up in thinking about Lacey that he didn't pay as much attention as he should to the cards and bet too high on a possible straight that didn't pan out. He was lucky in that Dandy Dan was bluffing and didn't have anything, either. High card won the hand and he had an ace to Dan's king.

Fargo buckled down. Against a professional like Dan he couldn't afford another mistake.

He seldom bluffed much, himself. Bluffs worked best against green players. Seasoned players were too skilled at reading tells.

They seesawed back and forth, winning and losing, until the clock above the bar was pushing eight o'clock at night.

Fargo was dealt three queens. Dandy Dan opened. Fargo slid his chips in and asked for two cards; he got two fours. Dandy Dan had asked for two cards, too, and now he raised.

Fargo smiled and said, "If you want this one you have to go all in." And he did.

Dandy Dan studied him. "I've noticed you don't bluff much but this could be the one time you try."

"It'll cost you to find out," Fargo said. He didn't really expect Dan to fall for the trap.

"Do you know what I think? I think you are. I think you save your bluffs for late in the game. By then you've set a pattern and it can win you more than you lose."

"Do you really want to go all in to find out?"

Dandy Dan did.

They compared cards.

"I'll be damned," Dandy Dan said. He had a full house, too; eights and twos.

Fargo raked in his winnings.

"I overthought it, didn't I?" Dan said, apparently to himself. Dan rose and offered his hand. "If you played for a living you'd live like a king."

"No, thanks," Fargo said. As much as he liked poker, playing cards day in and day out for the rest of his life would be dull. Poker was like whiskey, and for that matter, women, in that the times he went without made him appreciate the times he drank, played, and made love that much more.

The other tables were winding down. Lacey was still in. So was Vin Creed.

Fargo stretched and rose and walked over to the bar. He was taking his first sip when the senator joined him.

"Well done. I'd have given odds Dan would be in it at the end."

"It could have gone either way."

Deerforth glanced at the clock. "It's late. No need for you to sit in on another table. Call it a day and start fresh in the morning."

"Fine by me," Fargo said. He had something to do. He polished off the rest of his drink in two swallows and went out.

He went around to the side of the saloon and stood in the shadows with his hands on his Colt.

After Dan's revelation, he'd kept an eye out for Jules but hadn't seen him go by the window. He couldn't see why Dandy Dan would lie, so either Jules had stopped peeking in at him or had been more careful about it.

The horizon swallowed the sun and the shadows darkened. Jules didn't appear.

Disappointed, Fargo went back in. The games were done for the day. Lacey and Vin were drinking at the bar. He plastered a smile on his face and went over.

"I don't want another drink spilled on me," Lacey said.

"Can't blame me for being mad after what you pulled," Fargo said. "But to show you there are no hard feelings, I'll treat you to a bottle."

Lacey arched an eyebrow. "What are you up to?"

"Trying to be nice."

"Now I've heard everything," Creed said. "Skye Fargo has turned Quaker."

Fargo could have kicked him.

"Not that I won't accept your generosity," Lacey said. "It's the least you can do. I wiped off that drink you dumped on me but I've felt sticky all damn day."

"I like it when a woman is sticky," Creed said. "It shows she's interested."

"The things that come out of your mouth," Lacey said.

"It's the things that go in that I like." Creed grinned and winked.

"You wouldn't think it was so funny if he'd dumped that drink on you."

"Poor baby," Vin Creed said.

"Maybe not so poor by this time tomorrow. That one hundred thousand will do me just fine."

"You have to beat me to win it and that's not going to happen," Creed assured her.

"Keep dreaming," Lacey taunted.

Fargo turned his back to the bar and leaned on his elbows. Most of the spectators had left and the saloon was quiet save for the clink of glasses and the murmur of conversation. He looked at Lacey. "I hear you like sailors."

Her puzzlement seemed genuine. "Care to explain that?"

"Short man, a lot of muscle, you were talking to him a few nights ago."

"I was?"

"So I heard." Fargo didn't elaborate.

"I talk to a lot of men."

"So you don't know him? His name is Jules."

"Jules?" Lacey said, her forehead puckered. "No, I don't re—" She stopped. "Oh, wait. There was a rude little runt who propositioned me the other night. Came right up and asked me how much it would cost. Can you imagine? The nerve of some people."

"The way you dress, you can't blame him," Vin Creed said.

Lacey's cheeks became pink. "What's wrong with how I dress?"

"Nothing at all, my dear," Creed said. "I love it when a woman's tits try to jump into my mouth."

"You're despicable."

Creed laughed. "My dear woman, you have no idea."

15

On the way to the mansion Fargo suspected he was being followed. He didn't see anyone behind him. He didn't hear another horse. But he still had a sense that someone was back there. Twice he drew rein at the side of the road and waited but no one appeared.

The mansion was lit up bright. The Deerforths were entertaining and parked carriages lined the gravel loop for a hundred yards.

Fargo stripped the Ovaro and fed it oats. He was heading out of the stable when someone whispered his name above him.

It was Roselyn, on her hands and knees at the edge of the hayloft. "What are you doing up there, girl?"

"Not so loud," she said, grinning. "I don't want anyone to know I'm out here." She beckoned. "Come on up."

Fargo reminded himself she was only fourteen and said, "Another time. I figured I might turn in early."

"Please. I want to talk to you."

By the time Fargo reached the top of the ladder she was over by the loft door, peeking out at the mansion. He walked over and hunkered. "What are you up to?"

"I'm spying on the people who are coming and going."

Fargo would have thought she was a little old for such nonsense. All he said was, "Having fun?"

"Oh, I'm not doing it for that. I want to prove to Garvin that I was right and he's wrong."

"About what?"

"The man I saw staring in my bedroom window."

As Fargo recollected, her room was on the second floor. "Did he sprout wings and fly up?"

"Very funny," Roselyn said, not sounding at all amused.

"But I saw him clear as anything. About two hours ago, it was. I was at my desk writing in my diary and I looked over and he was staring in at me. It gave me a frightful start."

"What did you do?"

"When I collected my wits I went over but he wasn't there. I ran downstairs to tell my mother and saw Garvin so I told him. We went outside and under my window. There wasn't anyone around."

"Did Garvin have the grounds searched?"

"He didn't think there was any need. He refused to believe me. He said that someone would need a ladder to get to my window and a ladder would leave marks and there weren't any. He said I must have imagined it."

Fargo was inclined to agree with Garvin. "What did this man look like?"

"All I saw was his face and shoulders. He had dark hair and a funny little cap."

"Cap?"

"Yes. You know, one of those small round caps like seamen wear. I forget what they call them."

Fargo was all interest. "What about the man himself?"

Roselyn shrugged. "He had dark hair and dark eyes. Oh, and his teeth stuck out."

"Buckteeth?"

"I think that's what they call them, yes."

Fargo sat back and tried to make sense of it. The description fit Ranson. But why would Ranson stare in the girl's window? Was he some sort of Peeping Tom? Some men got excited by that sort of thing.

"Do you believe me or are you like Garvin?"

"I believe you," Fargo said.

"You do?" Roselyn clasped her hands and squealed in delight. "Thank you. Maybe you can help me convince Garvin."

"You shouldn't be out here," Fargo said. "If that man is still around, it's not safe."

"Do you think he wants to harm me?"

"I have no idea what he's up to," Fargo admitted. "But it sounds like one of the men who is out to kill me."

"Oh my," Roselyn said.

"That's putting it mildly." Rising, Fargo held out his hand. "Let's go. I'm taking you in. Then I'll have a look around."

The first floor of the mansion was packed with people.

The Deerforths loved to entertain, and when the legislature wasn't in session, they held several social events each month.

Fargo and Roselyn were starting up the stairs when someone called Roselyn's name, and Ginny swept out of the parlor wearing a dress fit for a queen.

"My dear child, where have you been?" she said, embracing her daughter. "I've had Garvin looking all over for you."

"I went out for some air, Mother," Roselyn said.

Ginny held her at arm's length. "You shouldn't go traipsing off without telling me."

"I'm nearly grown," Roselyn said. "Surely I can go for a walk whenever I want?"

"Of course, child, of course." Ginny kissed her on the cheek. "But it's getting late and you should be in bed."

"That's where I'm heading."

Ginny straightened and put her hand on Fargo's arm. "And you, my dear friend. You'll join me in the parlor?"

"In a while maybe," Fargo said.

Ginny motioned at the talking, smiling people. "Marion lives for these affairs. He loves to socialize. Part of the reason he's in politics, I suspect." She turned. "Well, I suppose I better mingle. See you later."

Fargo led Roselyn upstairs. At the landing she stopped and frowned.

"Mother and Father might like these affairs but I don't. All the noise and the liquor. I can do without that, thank you very much."

"I thought girls your age love parties."

"One or two a year I wouldn't have a problem with," Roselyn said. "But thirty or more is a little much." She held out her hand. "Thank you for believing me. Please let me know what you find."

Fargo promised he would. He went downstairs and along the hall to the kitchen. Helping himself to a lamp, he went out the back door and around until he was under the girl's window. Sinking to one knee, he examined the grass. He noticed that in two spots the grass was flattened as if by a heavy weight. He could be wrong, but it looked to him as if a ladder *had* been put there. And whoever did it had wrapped pieces of cloth or burlap around the bottom so the edges wouldn't dig into the dirt.

"I'll be damned," Fargo said.

16

The senator was in the parlor, a drink in one hand and a cigar in the other, regaling his constituents, and he didn't appear particularly happy when Fargo nudged him and said that they needed to talk in private. Deerforth excused himself and ushered Fargo to a far corner.

"Why so somber, my friend? Don't tell me there's been another attempt on your life?"

"No," Fargo said, and explained about Roselyn and the face at her window and the flattened grass.

Deerforth tipped the glass to his mouth, and frowned. "Let me be sure I understand this. You seriously believe that one of the men who tried to murder you was spying on my daughter?"

Fargo nodded.

"To what purpose? How is she involved?"

"I wish to hell I knew."

"On the face of it, it seems preposterous." Deerforth gnawed his lower lip. "Then again, I can't afford to ignore it. I'll have Garvin post a man outside below her room. That should discourage whoever they are. Now if you'll excuse me." He walked off to find the overseer.

Fargo made his way to the stairs. As his hand fell on the banister, a hand fell on his shoulder.

"Where are you off to, handsome?" Lacey Mayhare had a drink and a tipsy smile on her pretty face.

"What do you want, bitch?"

Lacey took a step back. "Here now. Is that any way to talk to someone you've shared your bed with?"

"You do remember handcuffing me to the bedpost?"

"Don't tell me you're still upset? Goodness, you hold a grudge." Lacey laughed and smacked his arm. "Come on. I'll get you a drink."

"No." Fargo started up again but she snatched his sleeve. "Let go."

"Haven't you ever heard the expression, 'eat, drink and be merry'?"

"You played me for a sucker last night. It won't happen twice."

"I apologize, all right? It's not as if you were hurt by it."

Fargo placed his hand on her shoulder and looked her in the eyes. "Lacey, when I call you a bitch, I mean it. You think of yourself first and everyone else last. You lie. You cheat."

"So?"

"So I'd be a jackass to make the same mistake twice. Go find someone else to toy with. I don't want anything more to do with you."

"Aren't you mister high and mighty? I have half a mind to punch you."

"But you won't."

"Why not?"

"I'll punch back and I hit a lot harder."

Lacey sniffed and tilted her nose into the air and marched into the parlor.

"Good riddance." Fargo said to himself. He climbed to Roselyn's room and knocked on the door.

She asked who it was and opened it a crack. She was bundled in a robe.

"I was just about to turn in."

Fargo told her about his find, and that her father was posting a guard.

"Thank you, Skye," she said in obvious relief. "I can't wait to tell Garvin I was right."

"Keep your door bolted, just in case," Fargo advised.

Roselyn opened the door wider and reached out and squeezed his hand. "I do so like you," she said. "You're a lot nicer than everyone says."

"Hell." Fargo went around the corner and along an adjoining

49

hallway to his own room. He was ready for sleep. Tomorrow was the last day of the tournament and he needed to be sharp. He was about to open his door when someone called to him and Virginia Deerforth bustled up.

"Here you are. I wanted to talk to you in person. Marion just told me about the man at my daughter's window."

"I don't know any more than I told him," Fargo informed her, and thinking that was the end of it, he gripped the latch to go in.

"Wait," Ginny said. "You can't imagine how upset I am. Roselyn is everything to me."

"You're a good mother," Fargo said, but she didn't seem to hear him.

"I had her late in life, as you well know. It wasn't easy, let me tell you. There were complications and for a while the doctor feared I might lose her."

Fargo didn't want to hear this. "Ginny—"

"They had to cut me. I was near delirious from the pain and my life was in danger. They were afraid the ordeal of giving birth would kill me."

"Ginny," Fargo said again.

"You're a man so you have no idea what it was like. My first and only ever child. The doctor said I can never have another. And after all those years of trying. Marion and I never did find out if it was him or me. That I finally became pregnant surprised him immensely." Ginny stopped and seemed to be gazing into far distances. Then, smiling anxiously, she said, "What was I talking about?"

"You should go lie down," Fargo suggested.

"I can't. I have my hostess duties." Ginny wrung her hands. "I'm sorry to be such a bother. I don't have many people I can talk to and you listen so well." She turned to go but paused. "It's not as if we always have a choice, is it? Life forces us against our will. Given our druthers, a lot of us would live differently than we do."

"I have no idea what you're talking about."

Ginny smiled. "I'm sorry, again. I do tend to blather when I'm flustered. Chalk it up to an old woman's eccentricities. Good night and sweet dreams."

Fargo watched her walk off. He shook his head in be-musement and opened the door. The bedroom was dark. He'd left the lamp lit and figured the maid had extin-guished it when she tidied up. He left the door open and took a step toward the table—and an arm looped around his throat.

17

Fargo got a hand up and grabbed the arm and glimpsed the glint of steel. He seized his attacker's wrist and stopped the tip from slicing into his chest. Before he could throw the man off, a foot hooked him behind his leg and he was tripped and flung to the floor. His attacker held onto his throat. He rolled, or tried to.

"Got you this time," the man hissed in his ear.

Fargo recognized the voice; it was Jules. He heaved upward but couldn't break free. The knife inched closer. Twisting, he rammed his elbow into Jules's ribs. It had no effect. He did it again, and a third time, and Jules grunted and his grip slackened. Not a lot but enough that Fargo sucked in a breath.

Fargo knew that Jules's face was right behind him; tucking his chin, he rammed his head straight back. Jules cried out and wet drops spattered Fargo's neck. With both hands he grabbed Jules's knife arm at the wrist and wrenched with all his strength. There was a *crack*. Again Jules cried out, and the knife fell to the floor. Jules's other arm was still around Fargo's throat but it didn't stop Fargo from twisting and smashing his elbow against Jules's jaw. Jules released him and scrambled to recover the knife.

"Not this time," Fargo said. He drew and fired as Jules gripped the hilt, fired as Jules spun toward him, fired as Jules raised the blade. The last slug caught Jules in the forehead.

Jules's sailor's cap and a lot of hair and gore sprayed the quilt.

The body pitched over with a thud.

Fargo sat on the bed. If he hadn't gotten his hand up in time he'd be the one lying there bleeding like a stuck pig.

Shouts rose from all quarters. Feet pounded, and Senator Deerforth yelled, "Where did those shots come from?"

Someone must have told him because Deerforth filled the doorway. "My word," he blurted. "Are you all right?"

"Never better," Fargo said.

"Is he—?" The senator entered and pressed a finger to Jules's throat. "I should say he is. But what was he doing here?"

Fargo stared.

"No. You misunderstand," Deerforth said. "What I really want to know is how he got into your room?"

Of more interest to Fargo was how Jules knew *which* room he was in.

"I shudder to think he just walked into my home without anyone seeing him."

The hall was jammed. Ginny squeezed through the press, took one look, and turned away with a gasp of horror.

Garvin Oster loomed behind her, a revolver strapped around his waist. "I was out at the stable and heard shots." He came in and stood over the body and looked at Fargo. "This makes, what, the third time he tried to kill you? You must have been born under a lucky star, mister."

Senator Deerforth faced those peering in. "I'll have to ask all of you to go back downstairs."

When no one moved, Garvin waded into them. "You heard the senator. Clear the hall."

Some muttered but they went.

"We'll have to leave the body where it is for right now," Senator Deerforth said. "I'll send for the marshal. He should be here inside of an hour and we can get to the bottom of this."

Fargo doubted it. He began to reload.

"I must say, you're terribly calm for a man who has just taken a life."

"I'm going to take a couple more."

"What makes you say that?"

Fargo nodded at the body. "He had a pard. And someone put them up to it."

"You can't just up and kill them." Deerforth was going to say more but his wife reappeared, pale as a sheet, her fingers splayed over her bosom. "Virginia, dear, you shouldn't be in here."

Ginny ignored him. She stepped to the dead man and touched his arm with the toe of her shoe. "Just like that," she said.

"Come away." Deerforth put his arm over her shoulders, only to have her shake it off. "What *is* the matter with you?"

"He's dead."

"Yes, we can see that. He tried to murder Fargo and got his comeuppance. It's nothing to be distraught about."

Tears welled in Ginny's eyes. "An hour ago he was a living, breathing human being."

"Yes, well, if he wanted to go on breathing, he shouldn't go around trying to kill people."

"He was alive," Ginny said, "and now he's not."

Senator Deerforth glanced at Fargo and tapped a finger to his temple. He then placed his arm around his wife again. "You're befuddled, dear. The shock has gotten to you. I insist you let me take you to your room so you can rest. I'll have tea or warm milk brought."

Ginny looked at him, tears trickling down her cheeks. "Is this what we've come to, Marion?"

"Who, my dear? You're not making sense."

She turned to Fargo. "I don't blame you. You were only defending yourself. We do what we have to. Isn't that right?"

"Ginny, please." Deerforth guided her out, saying over his shoulder, "Sorry about this. Keep watch over the body, would you, until the marshal gets here?"

"It's not going anywhere," Fargo said.

18

The marshal didn't get done with his questions and haul off the body until nearly three.

Fargo turned in but couldn't sleep. His mind wouldn't shut down. It kept trying to come up with answers but he didn't even know the right questions. Along about five he drifted off and not two hours later was awakened by a sound out in the hall.

Struggling to sit up, Fargo shook his head to clear it. He stumbled to the basin, filled it with the pitcher of water that was always kept handy, and dashed some on his face. It didn't help. He dressed and strapped on his Colt and went down to the kitchen. The cook was a plump woman by the name of Maria. She fixed him five eggs with strips of bacon and toast and put on a fresh pot of coffee.

Six cups later Fargo felt half human. He was still sluggish, though, and that could cost him at the card table. It would be nice if Deerforth was willing to postpone the tournament a day but that wouldn't happen. Another of the rules was that the games wouldn't be delayed for any reason whatsoever. He was almost done when someone came skipping and humming down the hall and grinned in delight at seeing him.

"Skye! Good morning."

Roselyn hugged him and went over to the cook and hugged her and kissed her on the cheek. The girl wore a gorgeous white dress with a lot of bows and frills that made her look younger than she was. She had on matching white shoes. "Isn't it a beautiful morning?"

"If you say so," Fargo said.

"My, aren't you the grumpy drawers?" Roselyn laughed.

"Why aren't you more happy? Today you could win my father's tournament and have all that money."

"You didn't hear about last night?"

Roselyn had accepted a glass of orange juice from Maria and was about to take a sip. She stopped, and lost her smile. "Oh. That's right. But you killed him. Aren't you safe now?"

"There's another one running around somewhere," Fargo reminded her. "The one who peeked in your room."

"Oh," Roselyn repeated, and frowned. "Well, now you've spoiled my good mood."

"You be careful until I can get to the bottom of this," Fargo advised.

"Do you think you can?"

"Only a matter of time." Fargo noticed that Virginia had come in and was listening, her face as pale as the night before. "Morning."

"Mother!" Roselyn exclaimed, and gave Ginny a hug and a kiss, too.

"I wish we wouldn't discuss that terrible business so early in the day," Ginny said. "My constitution can't take it."

"Doesn't help to bury our heads in the sand," Fargo said. "Things like this don't go away on their own."

"Why wouldn't it?" Ginny said. "You killed one of them. Maybe they'll give up."

Fargo took a swallow of coffee. He had been thinking about it, and he disagreed. "They've been after me for days. Whatever they're up to, it's important enough that they snuck into your home when it was full of guests and tried to make worm food of me. They won't give up."

"You think you know what they're up to?"

"I didn't say that," Fargo said. "But whatever it is, they made the biggest mistake they could."

"Which was?"

"I don't take kindly to someone trying to stick a knife in me. I'm going to find out who is behind this and repay the favor."

"That's terribly brutal of you."

"And what do you call the bastard who tried to knife me? He was no daisy."

"Please, Skye, my daughter is present. Your language, if you don't mind."

"Hell," Fargo said.

"I'd like to know what those men are up to, too," Roselyn said. "Why in the world was one of them looking in my window? It makes no sense."

"It makes sense to them," Fargo said.

Ginny closed her eyes and put a hand to her forehead. "I never counted on anything like this in my life."

"Who ever does?" Fargo said.

"I see your point. I have everything a person could ask for. A fine home, a child I adore, a husband who is devoted to us, and now this."

Fargo didn't think she saw the point at all but he didn't say so.

Ginny shook herself. "Well, today is the big day. By this time tonight maybe it will all be sorted out."

"I doubt it," Fargo said. "I have a lot of poker to play before I can go after Ranson and whoever is behind this."

"How very fortunate for them," Ginny said.

19

Only six of the original twenty players were left. Fargo, Vin Creed, Lacey Mayhare, Sly Jackson, the Mississippi Riverboat gambler, a man named Clark who had come all the way from San Francisco, and Billy Banks, an older man who had been most everywhere and done most everything and was a wizard with cards.

Instead of all of them sitting down at one table and going at it, the senator paired them off by drawing lots.

Fargo found himself pitted against Sly Jackson, a tall, slim, quiet gent who took his cards seriously and seldom spoke while he was playing. For over three hours they waged war. Then, on Fargo's deal, Jackson wagered half his chips. Fargo figured it wasn't a bluff. But Jackson didn't know that he had an ace-high straight. It might not be enough but Fargo called and won. On the very next hand Jackson went all in. Fargo had two pair, kings and tens. He was suspicious of the raise. Some players, after a big loss, resorted to a bluff to try and recoup their losses. Supposedly, Jackson was professional enough not to give in to the temptation. Then again, even a professional made mistakes. Fargo took a deep mental breath, and called.

Jackson had two pair, as well: queens and threes.

Fargo smiled as he added the chips to his growing mountain.

At the table across from him, Creed had cleaned out Clark. Lacey was still battling Banks.

Fargo raised his empty glass so the bartender could see it and the man brought a refill. As he was sipping and relaxing, a chair scraped and Vin Creed sank down.

"Could end up being you and me."

"It could," Fargo said.

"What will you do with all that money?"

"Haven't thought that far ahead."

"I have," Creed said dreamily. "I'm not touching it. I'm socking it away and saving it until I'm too old to shuffle cards."

"You can do that?" Fargo said. For most gamblers, it was easy come, easy go. Money slipped through their fingers like water.

Creed grinned. "I can try."

There was a loud squeal of pure joy and Lacey Mayhare stood up and whooped.

"I was hoping Banks would beat her," Creed said.

It was down to the three of them. Senator Deerforth put slips of paper with their names into a hat and drew two of the slips out. They would duel, and whoever won would face the last contender.

Fargo would rather have all three of them sit down and slug it out but it was the senator's tournament and Deerforth liked to draw the play out as long as he could, as much for the entertainment as for the money the saloon took in.

Now the senator read the slips. "Vin Creed and Lacey Mayhare," he announced.

Vin and Lacey chose a table and Lacey dealt.

Fargo reckoned he had a few hours to kill. Neither would go down easy. He went outside and leaned against a post and gazed up and down the street and spotted Ranson two blocks down on a bench by the butcher's. Ranson must have been watching the Cosmopolitan but at the moment he was distracted by a pair of lovely ladies sashaying by the bench.

Fargo moved close to a buckboard that was clattering past and crouched so he couldn't be seen. Keeping the buckboard between him and the butcher's, he closed on his quarry.

Ranson said something to the women and one of them laughed and they walked on. He stared at the saloon and idly rubbed his chin.

Fargo put his hand on his Colt. The marshal would have a fit if there was gunplay in the street but he was going to get to the bottom of this, here and now.

The buckboard was almost abreast of the butcher's. The farmer in the seat glanced down and loudly blurted, "Hey, mister. What are you doing down there? Who are you hiding from?"

Ranson heard, and looked over.

With an oath, Fargo darted around the end of the wagon but Ranson was already up and running. Fargo gave chase and they pounded past the general store and a tailor's. Ranson came to an alley and darted into it. Fargo recklessly followed suit and nearly paid for his folly with his life. A pistol cracked and lead bit into the wall inches from his head. Fargo raised the Colt but Ranson sped out the other end of the alley.

"Damn."

Fargo flew. When he came to the end he stopped and poked his head out. Another shot nearly clipped his hat. He brought the Colt up but once again Ranson thwarted him by flying up a side street.

Shouts were erupting. Soon the law would come.

Fargo needed to end it quickly. He sprinted to the side street. Ranson wasn't in sight. Fargo peered into windows, looked into doorways. People got out of his way, mothers clutching their small children, men with hands in their pockets or inside their jackets.

Ahead was a hotel. It had a balcony on the second floor. How Ranson got up there, Fargo would never know, but as he neared it, a shadow reared and two shots banged. Fargo felt a slight sting in his left shoulder; he had been nicked. He was passing a horse trough and threw himself flat and got off a shot of his own but the shadow had disappeared.

People yelled and a woman screamed and a lot of pedestrians were running or had dropped to the ground.

Taking his hat off, Fargo inched an eye to the end of the trough. The balcony seemed empty but he couldn't see all of it. He inched out farther. Ranson popped up and fired, and Fargo nearly lost an eye to exploding slivers. He slid back.

Inside the hotel, a woman screeched in fear.

Fargo grabbed his hat and ran to the entrance. He threw himself inside and to the right of the doorway. Upstairs, feet pounded. "Is there another way out?" he hollered at the petrified clerk.

The man nodded and pointed at a narrow hall.

Fargo raced to it and saw Ranson going out the other end. He didn't slow. He figured Ranson would keep on running. But as he cleared the threshold a foot was thrust in front of his legs and he pitched headfirst to the dirt.

20

Fargo started to rise and turn. Out of the corner of his eye he saw Ranson bending, a Starr revolver pointed at his head. Ranson was smiling, thinking he had him, thinking there was no way Fargo could turn and shoot before Ranson squeezed the trigger. And he was right. But Fargo didn't turn and shoot. His Colt was already pointing in Ranson's direction, belly high—all he had to do was fire.

At the blast Ranson cried out and staggered. Colliding with the wall, he clutched his stomach. Blood pumped between his splayed fingers. He looked down, aghast, and said breathlessly, "No."

Fargo leveled the Colt. "I want a name."

Ranson oozed to the ground, his legs too weak to support him. "What?" he said, still staring at the wound and the blood.

"The name of whoever hired you and your pard, and why they want me dead."

"Bastard," Ranson said.

"The name or I'll shoot you again."

Ranson had dropped the Starr. He saw it and gritted his teeth and lunged.

Fargo kicked it away.

"Bastard, bastard, bastard," Ranson hissed. Shutting his eyes, he groaned.

"The name."

"Go to hell."

"You first." Fargo extended the Colt and thumbed back at the hammer.

At the *click* Ranson looked up. "Jules was more than my partner. He was my cousin."

"Being stupid must run in your family."

Red beads trickled from the corner of Ranson's mouth.

"I won't tell you a thing. Finish me off. It won't stop it. Nothing can stop it."

"Stop what?"

"Not a word more." Ranson bowed his head and shuddered. "I'm so damn cold."

"I'll get you to a doc if you tell me."

"We were to get five thousand for you," Ranson said weakly. "That was our share."

"Share of what?"

Ranson uttered a bitter bark. "Jackass. It's right in front of you and you don't see it. But then, he doesn't either, does he?"

"Make sense," Fargo said.

A grim grin curved Ranson's bloody lips. "You were a precaution. Can you believe that? My cousin and me, dead, and you might not even be as good as they say you are."

"Good how?"

Ranson sank onto his side and commenced to quake. More scarlet mixed with spittle dribbled down his chin. "So . . . cold . . ." he said through chattering teeth.

"Damn you." Fargo resisted an urge to kick him. He'd hoped to end this. Now whoever was behind it was immune from his vengeance and free to try to kill him again.

Ranson uttered a low gurgle. "You think you beat me but I beat you."

Fargo tried a different tack. "Why were you looking in the girl's window?"

"The girl," Ranson said. "Wouldn't have hurt her. It's for the best."

"What is?"

Ranson would never answer. His eyes went wide and his mouth went slack and his chest stopped moving.

"Just my luck," Fargo said, and tensed at the ratchet of a rifle lever behind him.

"Keep your hands where I can see them," Marshal Moleen said, "or I will by God splatter your brains."

"This is the other man who was trying to kill me," Fargo said.

"We'll sort that out," the lawman said. "In the meantime, set down that six-gun of yours, real slow."

Moleen wasn't alone. He had a nervous deputy. While the deputy dealt with the body, Moleen took Fargo to his office and questioned him. Fargo had to go over everything from the time he came out of the saloon and saw Ranson on the bench.

"So he took the first shot?" Moleen wanted it clarified.

"Ask around if you don't believe me," Fargo said. There were bound to be witnesses.

"Don't think I won't."

Fargo was puzzled. "Why are you acting like I'm to blame? You already know about the tries on my life."

Marshal Moleen leaned back in his chair. "I don't like killings in my town. Thanks to you, I've had two in two days. You say they were out to get you. That may well be, but I only have your word on it."

"Why else did Jules sneak into my room?"

"If he did," Moleen said. "For all I know, the two of you were in cahoots and had a falling out."

Fargo was about to say that was damned stupid but held his tongue. "Listen. We can talk this out whenever you want. But I have to get back to the saloon. The games are still going on and if I'm not there when my name's called, I lose out."

"That's too bad," Marshal Moleen said, "because you're not going anywhere until I say." He smiled a cold smile. "Now then, suppose you take it from the beginning again."

21

It was almost an hour before Senator Deerforth showed up.

He listened to the marshal's account of the affair, and he wasn't happy. "Why are you treating Fargo as if he's the culprit? I made it plain he's my friend, didn't I?"

Marshal Moleen tapped his badge. "You see this? The law should be the same for everybody. I treat him as I'd treat any hombre."

"He had a poker game to take part in."

"So he reminded me," Moleen said. "But the law comes first."

Senator Deerforth gave Fargo an apologetic look and turned back to the lawman. "Must you be such a stickler?"

Moleen sighed. "Take him if you want. No charges will be filed."

"I thank you, Floyd," Deerforth said.

"Just doing my job, Marion." The marshal held out Fargo's Colt.

Fargo twirled it into his holster. He wasn't in the best of moods and slammed the door on his way out.

"I understand your feelings." Deerforth commiserated.

"Took you long enough to show up," Fargo said.

"I came as soon as I was able," Deerforth replied. "I couldn't very well walk out when Mr. Creed and Miss Mayhare were so close to the finish."

Fargo stopped and faced him. "It's over?"

"I'm afraid so."

"Who?" Fargo asked.

"Miss Mayhare. Mr. Creed went all in with a full house. Miss Mayhare had four of a kind."

"Damn," Fargo said.

"I'm sorry," Senator Deerforth went on. "I told her about your plight and I asked if she was willing to wait while I fetched you."

"She said no," Fargo guessed.

"She said no," Deerforth confirmed. "She insisted I abide by the rule that if a player is absent from play, they forfeit." He gestured, his palms out. "What else could I do? I formally declared her the winner."

"God, I need a drink," Fargo said, and bent his boots toward the saloon.

"Hold on." The senator caught up, taking two steps for each of his. "The bottle will be on me. It's the least I can do."

"Make it two bottles," Fargo said. He aimed to get good and drunk.

"As you wish." Deerforth fiddled with his cravat. "She did agree to wait for me to see about you before I turn the money over to her."

"She doesn't have it yet?"

"I'm giving it to her at a special ceremony." Deerforth smiled. "She's quite impatient to get it over with. You can't imagine how much she wants that hundred thousand."

"Yes," Fargo said. "I can." He slowed. "Nice day for a stroll, don't you think?"

Deerforth slowed too, and grinned. "We take too long, she'll be madder than a wet hen."

"Let's hope."

The senator laughed. "We'll tell her Marshal Moleen wouldn't let you leave."

"I'll tell her the truth," Fargo said.

"You *want* her mad at you?"

"After what she pulled?"

"She's an armful, I must admit," Senator Deerforth remarked. Realizing what he'd said, he quickly amended. "That came out wrong."

Fargo was thinking about Ranson and Jules. Whoever sent them might send others. It occurred to him that if he asked around down at the docks, someone might know something. He realized the senator was talking.

"—will attend. We're holding it out in front of the Citizens Banks of Deerforth, which I own, by the way."

"Is that wise?" Fargo wondered.

"Marshal Moleen and his deputies will be there to ensure no one lets temptation get the better of them. Garvin will be there, too, as he always is, with several men in my employ."

"You'll have a small army."

"It's been enough in other years," Deerforth said. "The outlaw element knows better than to try anything. You might not think much of Moleen but he has grit to spare and the criminals know it." Deerforth rose onto his toes and stared at a brick building. "Speak of my bank and there is it. Do you mind if we stop? I must inform the bank president that we'll be there to disperse the money within the hour."

Fargo followed the senator in and over to where a portly man in an expensive suit was scribbling in a ledger. The man glanced up when Deerforth cleared his throat.

"Senator! This is a surprise." The man smiled and rose and came around his desk.

"I just want to make sure all is in readiness for the ceremony, Benton," Deerforth said.

"I beg your pardon?" the banker said.

"The ceremony when we give the money to the winner. My God, man, how can you have forgotten?"

"It's not that," Benton said. "It's just that I'm terribly confused."

"What is there to be confused about?" Deerforth demanded.

"I've already handed the money over."

22

"What in God's name are you talking about?" Senator Deerforth said. "You gave the money to Lacey Mayhare without my say-so?"

"Lacey Mayhare?" Benton said. "No, I gave the money to your overseer, Garvin Oster."

"What?"

"I gave him the one hundred thousand," Benton said, "as you instructed."

Deerforth glanced in bewilderment at Fargo and then back at the bank president. "Explain, Mr. Benton, and explain quickly. Either you are incompetent or insane."

Benton drew himself up to his full height. "I am neither, Marion. We've been friends too long for you to talk to me like that."

"But my God, man, you gave Garvin the money?"

"He had a letter," Benton said. "In your handwriting. Signed by you. Instructing me to give the money to him."

"Letter? What letter?"

Benton went around his desk, opened a drawer, and took out a folded sheet. He gave it to Deerforth.

The senator read it aloud in a tone of disbelief. " 'Mr. Benton. This is to inform you there has been a change in plans. I have moved the ceremony from the bank to the Cosmopolitan. I do not have time to come over in person for the funds so I am sending Garvin. Please give the money to him and he will bring it to me. Most cordially, Marion Deerforth.' " Deerforth turned the paper over and looked at the other side and then read it again and when he looked up, he had a dazed expression. "This looks like my handwriting but it isn't. It's a forgery."

"Are you saying you didn't write that?"

"Do your ears work?" Deerforth angrily demanded. Controlling himself, he said, "I never changed anything. The ceremony is to be held here, not at the saloon."

"I don't understand," Benton said.

"That makes two of us. Garvin has been with me for years. I trust him as I do my wife. What can he possibly have been thinking?"

To Fargo it seemed obvious but he kept it to himself as Deerforth proposed going to the saloon and Benton offered to come along. Fargo trailed after them, listening to them speculate, and marveled that a senator and a banker could be so thick between the ears.

No sooner did they stride through the batwings than Lacey Mayhare came over showing more teeth than a patent medicine salesman. "Here you are, at last," she exclaimed. "Let's get this over with. My hands are itching for my money."

Senator Deerforth gazed about the saloon. "Garvin Oster isn't here?"

"Your foreman or whatever he is?" Lacey said. "No, I haven't seen him all day."

Vin Creed joined them. He had a half empty bottle and appeared well on his way to getting drunk. "Let's hear it for the winner," he said, and raised the bottle to Lacey.

"Will you stop?" she snapped. "I won. Get over it, you big baby."

"There is no God," Creed said, and chugged.

"He's been this way since you left," Lacey told the senator. "I've heard of poor losers but he's ridiculous."

"It's not the losing," Creed said. "It's losing to the likes of you."

"I won't be insulted," Lacey said.

"Then you shouldn't be a conniving bitch," Creed said. He chuckled and drank.

"I don't have time for this," Senator Deerforth said. Brushing past them, he went to the bar. "Tom, has Garvin Oster been in here this morning?"

"Garvin hasn't been in in days," the bartender said.

"I'm going home," Deerforth announced. "Garvin must have taken the money there."

"Hold on," Lacey said. "Your foreman has *my* money?"

"He's my overseer and my right hand and my good friend," Deerforth told her.

"That's nice," Lacey said, "but what is he doing with *my* money?"

"That's what I intend to find out."

"I'm going along. It's *my* money."

Benton wanted to go, too, and the three of them hastened out to the senator's carriage.

Fargo climbed on the Ovaro and followed. As they neared the end of the main street, a zebra dun overtook the stallion.

"I decided to tag along," Vin Creed said, and offered the bottle. "Care for a swig?"

Fargo allowed himself a swallow and passed the bottle back. "How well do you know Garvin Oster?"

"Not well at all," the gambler said. "I've seen him a few times and that's it." He swished the bottle. "I did hear he killed a man a long time ago, with his bare fists. Back before he came to work for the senator." He looked at Fargo. "Are you thinking what I'm thinking?"

"Could be," Fargo said.

"I can't wait to see the look on Mayhare's face."

When the carriage pulled up at the mansion, a servant came out to meet it, an older man with gray at the temples.

"James," the senator greeted him, "where's Garvin? I must speak with him immediately."

"He's not here, sir," the servant said.

"He hasn't come back from town?"

"Yes, he did, sir," the servant answered. "But he left again about an hour ago."

"With *my* money?" Lacey asked.

"I wouldn't know about that, ma'am," the servant said. "He left with Mrs. Deerforth."

The senator looked as if he had been struck by lightning. "Virginia went with him?"

"Yes, sir. On horseback. She had her traveling bag and she appeared to be awful upset. I thought it strange but it wasn't my place to say anything."

"This can't be," Deerforth said. "Where's Roselyn? Maybe she knows what is going on."

"Why, she went with them, sir."

The senator put both fists to his temples. "I can't believe what I'm hearing. What on earth is happening?"

"Seems to me," Vin Creed said, "that it's as plain as the nose on your face. Your right hand and good friend has stolen your money, your wife, and your kid."

23

Fargo was in the kitchen having coffee when Marshal Moleen entered, his spurs jangling.

The lawman pulled out a chair and motioned at Maria and she brought a cup and the pot over. As she poured, Moleen pushed his hat back on his head and scratched his chin. "A hell of a mess."

"And then some," Fargo said.

"I've known Garvin pretty near twenty years, ever since he came to work for the senator."

Fargo sensed that Moleen was leading up to something and let him ramble.

"Garvin hasn't given anyone a lick of trouble in all that time. He's not as rowdy as he used to be."

"Rumor has it he killed a man," Fargo said.

"He rode with a wild bunch when he was younger. The Grissom brothers. Ever heard of them?"

Fargo shook his head.

"As mean a brood as was ever born. They and several others, Garvin among them, thought they were the cocks of the roost. When they weren't drunk they were getting drunk. They'd fight anyone at the drop of a feather and they'd drop the feather."

"I've run into their kind," Fargo said.

"Garvin wasn't the worst of that outfit but he was in the thick of it. That rumor you mentioned? Garvin was sweet on a dance hall gal and one night this other feller danced with her and got rough when she wouldn't let him take liberties." Moleen swallowed coffee. "Garvin didn't like it so he knocked the other feller down. Next thing, they were going at it with their fists. This other gent was almost as big as Garvin and from what I hear they tore that dance hall up. Broke tables, broke chairs, smashed a mirror. Finally Garvin hit him so hard, it broke the feller's neck."

Fargo imagined the brute strength it took to do something like that. "How is it you know all this?"

"I sniffed around. Looking out for the senator's interests, you might say."

"Deerforth kept Garvin on anyway?"

"The senator felt everyone deserves a second chance." Moleen scowled. "And this is how Garvin repays him. I don't know what to make of it except that Garvin has gone back to his bad ways."

"Shouldn't you be after him?"

"That's why I came to see you. I'm organizing a posse and I'd like you to be part of it. From what folks say, you're a damn good tracker."

"The army thinks so."

"You've scouted for them, I hear." Moleen set his cup down. "What do you say? Are you in? Two deputies are coming along. So is the senator even though I advised against it. And Benton and that gambler and Lacey Mayhare."

"A woman on a posse?"

"Miss Mayhare keeps saying as how it's her money and the only way she'll stay behind is if I throw her behind bars."

"That sounds like Lacey."

"So long as she does as I say and doesn't get underfoot, we shouldn't have a problem." Moleen stood. "I need an answer. In or out?"

Fargo thought of Roselyn and how friendly she had been. "In," he said.

"Good. Can you be ready to ride in half an hour?"

"I'm ready now."

Moleen hitched at his belt. "Meet us out front. With a little luck we can settle this and be back here by this time tomorrow." He jangled out.

Fargo figured to finish his coffee in peace but someone else came strolling in.

"There you are. I've been looking all over for you," Vin Creed said.

"I hear you're going with the posse."

Creed sat in the same chair the lawman had used. "Deerforth asked me to."

"You're no manhunter."

"True," Creed said. "But Deerforth asked for a personal favor and I can't hardly say no. Not after how well he's treated me at his poker tournaments."

"What sort of favor?"

The gambler chuckled. "He took me aside and asked me to keep an eye on Lacey. Make sure she doesn't get underfoot, as he put it."

"Have you told her yet?"

"And have her bean me with a rock? No thank you. I'll keep it to myself, and I'd be obliged if you'd do the same."

"She won't hear it from me," Fargo promised.

Creed folded his arms on the table. "Tell me true. What do you make of all this?"

"I know I don't think much of hombres who abduct little girls."

"Roselyn's not so little but I take your point. It doesn't sit well with me, either." Creed paused. "Say, you don't suppose there's a connection, do you?"

"With what?"

"Those two men who tried to kill you. What were their names again? Ranson and Jules? Do you reckon they were in cahoots with Garvin Oster?"

"Cahoots how?" Fargo said.

"I don't know. It's just strange that they try to buck you out in gore about the same time that Garvin helps himself to one hundred thousand dollars and the senator's family."

Fargo hadn't even considered that but now that he did, he wondered if Creed might be on to something.

"Have you seen the two deputies?" the gambler asked.

"Not yet."

"Green as grass," Creed said. "Then we've got the senator and the banker and sweet little Lacey and me." He laughed. "Out of all of us, the marshal and you are the only two who know what they're doing."

Fargo hadn't considered that, either. "Hell," he said.

"Yes sir," Creed said, chuckling. "It will be a wonder if we don't get ourselves killed."

24

Fargo had to agree. As posses went, they were plumb ridiculous.

Apparently there was a reason Senator Deerforth took a carriage everywhere; he was the worst rider in Texas. He flopped. He bounced. He sat his saddle as if he were about to jump off it. And every time he drew rein, he hollered, "Whoa, boy, whoa."

Banker Benton wasn't much better. He didn't flop or bounce but he was incapable of sitting a saddle straight. Either he leaned to one side or the other and his legs were always bent at odd angles.

Lacey Mayhare could ride better than both, and outbitch everybody. She wouldn't stop complaining. About the heat. About the dust. About how her horse smelled of horse sweat. About how she was going to stick a dagger in Garvin Oster for stealing *her* money.

Vin Creed could ride, too. And drink like a fish. Whether it was because he lost the tournament or he was making up for lost time, every five minutes he sucked on one of the whiskey bottles he'd brought along.

The two deputies were as green as the gambler had claimed, but rode proud and tall and were eager to show what they were made of.

The posse was a mile out from the mansion when Fargo gigged the Ovaro up next to Marshal Moleen's buttermilk. "You should send the four of them back."

The lawman didn't ask which four. "As much as I would like to, I can't."

"You're wearing the badge."

Moleen touched the tin pinned to his vest. "I won't be for

long if I make the senator and a bank president mad at me. They're liable not to support me at the next election."

"They can't support you if they're dead, either."

"I'll keep an eye on them," Moleen said. "You do the tracking."

"That's what I'm here for," Fargo said.

"In fact," the lawman continued, "it would help if you pushed on ahead. You can cover twice as much ground as we can."

"More than that."

"Even better. And less chance of the senator and the banker coming to harm."

"You'll be able to follow me?"

"If you leave signs. Rocks to point the way and like that."

Fargo frowned. Stopping to leave sign took time he'd rather not lose. And sometimes there wasn't anything to leave a sign with—no rocks or tree limbs and the like. "I have a better idea. I'll find them and bring them back to you."

Now it was Marshal Moleen who frowned. "I'd rather you didn't tangle with Garvin Oster alone."

"I can handle him."

"He's tough, mister. Real tough."

"He's not the only one." Fargo tapped his spurs and brought the Ovaro to a gallop.

In one respect they were in luck. Oster had struck off cross-country instead of sticking to the roads. Not very smart on his part, Fargo reflected. On a road, tracks were mixed and jumbled with whoever and whatever went by before and after. On the open prairie, tracks stood out and were easy to follow. He reckoned he'd overtake the kidnapper and the ladies before an hour was out.

It bothered Fargo a little that they were holding to a walk. Oster should be riding like hell to get away. The man might be tough, as the marshal claimed, but he sure was dumb.

True to his prediction, in less than an hour Fargo spied stick riders on the horizon. He slowed and pondered. In open country he couldn't get close without being spotted. Either he waited until nightfall or he said to hell with it and caught up to them. He decided not to wait. He figured Oster would be overconfident and let him ride right up.

Fargo goaded the stallion to a trot. He was anxious to get

it over with and head back to town for a night of drinking and the company of a friendly dove. In the morning he would head north to the Teton country where he was to meet a trapper friend.

The stick figures had stopped.

Garvin Oster must have the eyes of a hawk, Fargo realized. He kept riding. He saw a stick figure separate from a stick horse and guessed that Oster had climbed down. Probably to wait for him. He kept riding. The man was overconfident, which would prove his undoing. There was a bright flash, as of the sun on metal, suggesting that Oster had shucked a rifle from his saddle scabbard. Fargo kept riding. He was too far off yet for any rifle to reach him except maybe a Sharps, and even if Oster owned one, it would take a damn good shot to hit him from half a mile off.

The next moment a slug whizzed past his head and thunder clapped in the distance.

25

Fargo had used a Sharps for years. He'd switched to a Henry because the Sharps was a single-shot and sometimes he got into scrapes where the Henry's fifteen rounds in the tube and one in the chamber meant the difference between breathing air and breathing dirt.

The Henry could spray a lot of lead but the Sharps could shoot a lot farther. An average shooter could hit a target at five hundred yards. A good shooter, a really good shooter, could better that by another five hundred.

Garvin Oster was better than good. From over half a mile away, he'd nearly taken Fargo's head off.

Fargo drew rein. He had a hunch that Garvin wasn't trying to kill him; it had been a warning shot. He took the warning to heart. Any closer, and the next shot wouldn't miss.

"Damn."

The stick figure on the ground climbed back on the stick horse and the three of them continued on.

Fargo had no choice. He must wait until dark and slip in after they made camp. When the three were almost lost in the haze, he resumed his pursuit. At a walk. Times like this, he regretted switching long guns. If he had his Sharps, he'd show Oster that he wasn't the only one who could drop a buff, or a man, from that distance.

Some time back Fargo had considered rigging a second scabbard so that he had the Henry on one side and the Sharps on the other. But that was a lot of bother to go to for the few times he'd use the Sharps, and he decided not to.

The sun was well on its westward arc. Another two to three hours and night would fall.

Fargo thought about Ginny and Roselyn. They must be

terrified, the girl in particular. Nothing like this had ever intruded on her life of ease and luxury.

Fargo gave some thought to Garvin Oster, too. After years of abiding by the law, for Oster to suddenly go bad like this was peculiar. He wondered what brought it on. Garvin had to know that any man who took women hostage would end up dangling from a rope.

The prairie gave way to rolling hills, and the tracks wound in among them.

Fargo rode with his hand on his Colt. He tried not to dwell on the fact that Oster could pick him off from ambush as easy as swatting a fly.

The shadows lengthened, the sun relinquished its reign of the heavens, and stars blossomed. The breeze picked up and brought with it the cries of coyotes and the hoot of an owl.

Fargo climbed the next hill he came to. At the crest he reined up and rose in the stirrups and spied what he was looking for: the orange and yellow glow of a campfire a mile or more away. It was careless of Oster to make the fire where it could be seen.

Fargo circled to come at them from the west. When he finally stopped again he was on top of another hill not two hundred yards from the fire. He dismounted, slid the Henry from the scabbard, and levered a round into the chamber.

As stealthily as an Apache, Fargo glided down the hill. He lost sight of the fire a few times. Fifty yards out he sank onto his belly and crawled.

As near as he could tell, the fire was in some sort of hollow or depression. The hollow was open to the south, which explained why he had seen it so clearly until he swung to the west. A low hump of earth screened him the final sixty feet.

He could hear the fire crackling. He didn't hear voices, and that puzzled him. It was too early for them to have turned in.

With utmost caution Fargo raised his head high enough to peer over. An oath escaped him. There was the fire—but nothing else. No Garvin Oster, no Ginny or Roselyn Deerforth, or their mounts.

It was a trick. Oster had used the fire to lure him in and once he showed himself, Oster would drop him with a bullet to the brain or the heart. But the longer Fargo lay there, the more the conviction grew that he was wrong, and Oster and the women were long gone. To test his hunch he took off his hat and waved it over his head. When that failed to provoke a response, he jammed it back on and hollered, "Garvin, it's Fargo. We need to talk."

From out of the dark, only silence.

Fargo was probing the night for movement when he caught sight of a square of white near the fire. A small piece of paper had been stuck on the split end of a stick and the stick had been jammed into the ground.

"What the hell?"

Fargo didn't go to it right away. He waited another ten minutes, then warily went down. His skin prickled with every step. But no shots boomed.

Hunkering, Fargo pried the paper loose and held it to the fire so he could read the note. It was in a neat feminine hand, the letters small and perfect. He read it through once and then a second time out loud. "'My dear Skye. Garvin says it is you who is after us although how he can tell from so far away amazes me. He wants me to tell you to go back. Leave us alone. He won't harm us. He gives you his word. Please heed him. I don't want bloodshed on my conscience. Your dear friend, Virginia Deerforth.'"

"Go back?" Fargo said, and laughed. Oster wouldn't get away that easy. If he had a say, Oster wouldn't get away at all.

26

Fargo went back up the hill to the Ovaro. He looked long and hard but couldn't spot another campfire. Either Garvin had made a cold camp or he'd kindled the fire where it couldn't be seen.

Temporarily thwarted, Fargo found a flat spot and settled in for the night. With his back propped on his saddle and his blanket pulled to his chest, he chewed on jerky and listened to the usual chorus of roving meat-eaters and the occasional bleat of prey.

Unless Garvin Oster pushed on through the night, Fargo figured they couldn't be more than a mile or two off. If he was up early enough and got to the top of a high hill, he might spot them.

With that hopeful thought Fargo drifted off. He slept soundly until the piercing scream of a cougar brought him to his feet with his Colt in his hand. The Ovaro snorted and stomped, a sure sign the cat was close. Fargo stayed awake until the stallion lowered its head and went back to dozing.

Thereafter, Fargo tossed and turned. He was up again well before sunrise. As a pink hue framed the eastern sky, he sat astride the stallion on a high hill, eager for a glimpse of the women and their abductor.

The pink changed to a blazing gold and a fiery crescent lit the world. Below Fargo the shadows shrank, giving way to the new day. He scoured the countryside and had about despaired of spotting them when his patience was rewarded.

Three riders were winding in single file to the northwest. By the size of the last rider, it was Garvin Oster.

"Got you." Fargo grinned and lashed the reins. He wanted

to reach them before they were out of the hills. In open country Oster would spot him from a mile off.

Fargo looped to the east and gave the Ovaro its head. His plan was to get ahead of them and give Oster the surprise of his life.

An hour and a half of hard riding brought Fargo to an ideal spot. He left the Ovaro in brush at the base of a bluff and moved around the bluff to a boulder. He was sure Oster and the women would pass close by. The chink of a shod hoof on rock proved him right. He heard voices but couldn't make out what they were saying. The first words he did understand were from Roselyn.

"I don't care what you say. I don't care what you want. I want to go home."

"Enough bellyachin', girl," Garvin Oster said. "I've had my fill of it."

"Now, now," Ginny said. "It would please me greatly if the two of you would stop this nitpicking."

"Mother," Roselyn said in exasperation. "He brought me against my will."

"I know, dear," Ginny replied, "but you're not helping matters by making him mad."

"Hug and kiss him, why don't you?" Roselyn said.

"Roselyn Deerforth," Ginny exclaimed. "That will be enough of that kind of talk."

They were near enough for Fargo to hear the creak of saddle leather. Tucking the Henry to his shoulder, he stepped from behind the boulder and centered the rifle's sights on Garvin Oster's chest. "Hold it right there."

"Skye!" Roselyn shrieked in delight.

All three drew rein.

"I'm so glad to see you!" Roselyn cried, and made as if to climb down.

"Not yet," Fargo said, and sidled a few feet to his right so he had a clear shot at Oster. "Everyone is to sit still. Except you, Garvin. Use two fingers and two fingers only and shuck your six-shooter."

"Go to hell."

"I have a lot to tell you," Roselyn said excitedly.

"Not *now*," Fargo stressed. He didn't dare let himself be distracted. His cheek to the Henry, he said, "Shuck it or die, Oster."

"He means it, Garvin," Ginny said.

"I won't go down easy," Oster said.

Fargo took a step closer. "I can't miss at this range."

"Shoot him," Roselyn urged.

"Hush, child," Ginny said, and twisted in her saddle to look at Oster. "Please, Garvin. I don't want your blood on my hands."

"It would be on his," Oster said, with a bob of his chin at Fargo.

"No. Make no mistake," Ginny said. "Whatever happens now is because of me." She turned to Fargo. "Please don't shoot him. Not on my account."

"It's his choice," Fargo said gruffly, annoyed that she was interfering.

"For me, Garvin." Ginny appealed to her captor.

Oster swore. Imitating a turtle, he plucked his revolver from his holster and let it fall to the ground. "There. Want me to drop my gun belt too?"

"No need," Fargo said. "Climb down, nice and slow." He covered him. "Now move away from your horse with your hands out from your sides."

"I'll get you for this, mister."

"Do it."

Glaring his spite, Garvin obeyed. "What now? You tie me and take me back?"

"Were it up to me I'd shoot you," Fargo said.

"Enough of that," Ginny intervened. "I'd like for all of us to get along."

"You're ridiculous, Mother," Roselyn said.

"That's no way to talk to your mother," Ginny said. "I demand an apology."

"Both of you be quiet," Fargo said. "Oster, lie on the ground and keep your hands where I can see them."

"I should have put that slug in your head," Garvin said, slowly sinking.

"You almost did."

"He wasn't trying to kill you," Ginny said. "I begged him not to."

Garvin was down, his arms outspread. "Where's Marion? Back at the mansion where he's safe?"

"Don't insult him," Ginny said. "It's unbecoming."

"You're not right in the head, Mother," Roselyn said. "You've gone insane."

Fargo had put up with all he was going to. He stroked the Henry's trigger.

27

At the blast, mother and daughter started.

Oster raised his head but showed no alarm. "What in hell did you do that for?"

Fargo had fired into the ground. He worked the lever and took aim. "To get everyone's attention. Not another damn peep out of any of you until I say so."

"Does that mean me too?" Roselyn asked.

"And me?" Ginny said.

"All of you."

"Why are you so mad?" Ginny asked. "We haven't done anything."

"Shut . . . the . . . hell . . . up."

Ginny raised a hand to her throat. "Well, I never. Here I thought we were friends."

"You really should let me tell you what I know," Roselyn said. "It's important."

"Not now, dear," Ginny said. "He's in a mood."

"But—"

Fargo glared at Roselyn and her cheeks flushed red and she clamped her mouth shut. In the few seconds he took his eyes off of Garvin Oster, Oster started to rise. Turning back, Fargo said, "You're not that quick."

Garvin sank down. "I'm quick enough. You'll find that out soon enough, by God."

Fargo went around Oster to Oster's horse and helped himself to a rope. He tossed it on the ground near Oster's legs.

"Tie your ankles. Do it good and tight."

"Like hell I will."

Fargo shrugged. "Either that, or I'll shoot you in the foot."

"You wouldn't," Ginny said.

Fargo ignored her. He was tired of her prattle. Wagging the Henry, he said to Oster, "I'll count to five and I'm already on four."

Garvin Oster was no fool. He slowly rolled over and slowly sat up and took hold of the rope. "You have no notion of what you're doin'."

"Says the jackass who stole a hundred thousand dollars and kidnapped two women."

"It's not what you think."

"You're stalling," Fargo said. "And like she said, I'm in a mood."

Oster looped one end of the rope around his ankles. "If Ranson and Jules had done what they were supposed to, you wouldn't be holding that rifle on me."

"They worked for you?"

Oster didn't answer.

Without being told to, Ginny dismounted. She brushed dust from her dress and fluffed her hair. "I haven't been out in the sun so much in years. It's not doing my skin any favors."

Fargo used to think she was a sweet old gal. But she was an idiot. "Has he hurt you in any way?"

"Garvin hurt me?" Ginny laughed. "Oh, please. He wouldn't harm a hair on my head."

"How about you?" Fargo asked Roselyn.

"You told us not to talk, remember?"

"It's all right to talk now," Fargo said, keeping one eye on Oster.

"I don't want to. You were rude."

"Save it for the marshal then," Fargo said.

Ginny put a hand to her throat. "Marshal Moleen is after us too?"

"What else did you expect? He organized a posse," Fargo said. "I'm part of it."

"Oh dear. Who else is with him?"

"Your husband. The banker. Lacey Mayhare and Vin Creed. And two deputies."

"Oh dear," Ginny said, and again, "Oh dear."

"I thought you'd be glad to hear it," Fargo said.

"I'd hoped they wouldn't come after us," Ginny said sadly. "Things haven't gone as they should."

Fargo's patience with her grew thinner by the minute. "You were abducted, for God's sake. Did you figure the law would overlook that? Or your husband would sit around twiddling his thumbs waiting to hear from you?"

"No, you don't understand." Ginny bowed her head and turned and took a few steps away from him.

Garvin Oster had two loops of rope around his ankles and was winding a third. "I have an idea," he said. "How about if I give you five thousand dollars and you let us go?"

"Keep trying."

"Ten thousand, then. That's a hell of a lot of money."

"And have the law after me? I'm not as dumb as you."

"No one would ever know," Garvin said. "Hide it in your saddlebags. Tell Moleen we gave you the slip."

"We?" Fargo said. "I'm taking Ginny and Roselyn back where they belong."

"You shouldn't have butted in," Garvin said. "We could have gotten clean away if not for you." He stopped winding. "All right. Twenty thousand, but that's as high as I'll go."

From behind Fargo, Ginny said, "That's too much."

Fargo hadn't heard her come up. Suddenly his head exploded in agony and a black pit yawned and he pitched into it and the world blinked out.

28

Pain brought him around.

Fargo lay still, collecting his senses. He was on his belly on the ground. His head throbbed. The back of his neck felt strange. Gingerly, he reached up. There was a gash as long as his little finger. Dry blood matted his hair and covered his neck.

"Son of a bitch."

He eased onto his side. His hat was next to him, partially crumpled. Wincing, he sat up. Ginny had hit him. He didn't know what to make of it; this whole damn business got crazier by the minute. He picked up his hat and reshaped it and carefully placed it on his head.

Judging by the sun, he had been unconscious for a couple of hours. He looked around. The women and Oster were long gone.

It was a wonder Garvin hadn't killed him.

Fargo put a hand down to prop himself so he could stand. He had to try twice. Swaying, he managed to stay up. He looked for the Henry but it wasn't there. He glanced at his holster; his Colt was gone, too.

Gritting his teeth, he walked slowly along the base of the bluff. The Ovaro was where he had left it, thank God. He climbed on and sat still until the waves of pain lessened.

Fargo rode back to where he had been struck. Their tracks led to the northwest. He resumed his pursuit, at a walk. He supposed he should be thankful he was still breathing. Oster had the perfect chance to kill him and hadn't. Was that Ginny's doing? But if so, why had she knocked him out?

The whole affair was a tangled knot that he was in no shape to unravel. He didn't bother to try. He rode until noon and stopped and rested. Seated on a flat rock, he chewed jerky and mulled over all that had happened since he arrived in Deerforth.

He recollected that Ranson and Jules had latched on to him almost as soon as he rode in. Since the pair worked for Garvin Oster, that told him two things. First, that Oster had been planning to steal the money for some time. Second, that Oster wanted him out of the way so he couldn't track him.

That still left the question of the women. Had Oster been planning to abduct them all along too? If so, why? Why not just steal the money and ride hell-bent for leather to parts unknown? The women slowed Oster down. They made escaping that much harder.

Fargo finished eating and climbed on the Ovaro. He'd find out what it was all about eventually. Oster had made another mistake in taking his guns and leaving him alive. He wasn't the forgive-and-forget type.

Evening came, and he hadn't caught up to them. They were pushing a lot faster. He debated riding into the night but decided to camp. His head could use the rest. He kindled a small fire and sat and ate more jerky and listened to the coyotes. He turned in early and had no trouble falling into an undisturbed sleep.

Dawn found him in the saddle again. He felt invigorated. His head was a little sore but not enough to bother him.

Toward the middle of the morning Fargo came to where Oster and the women had spent the night. They'd had a fire, too, and near the charred circle was another stick with a sheet of paper stuck to it, and next to the stick, placed neatly side by side, were his Henry and the Colt.

"I'll be damned."

Fargo dismounted. He inspected the rifle and the six-shooter, shoved the Henry into the scabbard, and plucked the note from the stick. Like the first, it was from Ginny. *"Dear Skye,"* it read. *"I pray you can forgive me. I am so very sorry. I would never hurt another living being but I'm afraid you left me no choice. I asked you before and I'll ask you again. Please go back. Please leave us be. There is more to this than you can imagine. All I can say for now is that I am not being held against my will. I have no need of rescue. Show this to my husband. Have him send the posse back. I don't want anyone else hurt. It's horrible enough that those two men are dead and you've been hurt. So far I've been able to persuade Garvin not to spill more blood but if you and the posse keep after us, I'm afraid I won't be able to restrain his more violent impulses. I've made him leave your weapons as a token of our good will. You have no other reason now to come after us. So please, again, go back. Your dear and devoted friend, Ginny Deerforth."*

Fargo read the note a second time. Ginny *wanted* to be with Oster? A dark suspicion came over him. He wouldn't have thought it possible, but then again, human nature being what it was, nothing surprised him. As for giving up and going back, Ginny was forgetting something: Roselyn. The girl was with them against her will.

Fargo put his hand on the Colt. "Go back my ass," he said.

He climbed on the Ovaro. Before the day was done he would end this, one way or the other.

The sun was past its zenith when he came on a ribbon of a creek. Oster had stopped to let their animals drink. By the sign they weren't more than an hour or so ahead.

Fargo squatted and dipped a hand in and sipped. He forked leather and crossed and went up a low bank and drew rein in consternation.

Four riders had come in from the west, discovered the tracks of Oster and the women, and gone off after them. The horses the four rode weren't shod. They were Indians, and if Fargo had to guess, he suspected they were from the tribe that some called the scourge of Texas. It was rare for them to be this far south but he was willing to bet good money the four were Comanches.

29

Fargo used his spurs. He didn't give a damn about Garvin Oster and he cared less about Ginny's fate than he had when he started out but there was Roselyn. The girl didn't deserve to spend the rest of her days in a Comanche lodge.

Comanches were superb riders and fierce fighters. They resented that the land they had roamed for more winters than anyone could remember was being taken by whites. Uncounted raids on farms, ranches, and even settlements had filled the white population with dread. Little mercy was shown by either side, which had Fargo worried the warriors wouldn't take Roselyn alive. It could be they'd kill her outright with the others.

Garvin Oster had been a fool to try to cross the prairie with only the women for company. Or maybe Oster thought it would deter others from coming after him. Ranson and Jules, the fake note to the banker, the best way to escape; a lot more planning had gone into this than anyone suspected.

Fargo's inclination was to push the Ovaro to the point of exhaustion, but he didn't. He might need to rely on the stallion's stamina later so he alternated between a trot and a walk.

The tracks became so fresh, he wasn't far behind. He shucked the Henry and held it across the saddle, ready for instant use.

Ahead stretched interminable prairie. Here and there islands of trees rose out of the sea of grass.

Fargo was considerably surprised when, along about four in the afternoon, he spied a gray tendril rising skyward from a cluster of cottonwoods. The tracks of Oster and the women led right to the stand.

The Comanches had split up, two veering to either side.
Fargo drew rein. The air was still, the prairie peaceful.

He hadn't heard shots so it could be the Comanches hadn't struck yet. The smart thing to do was climb down and crawl but he wasn't about to leave the Ovaro untended. Comanches loved to steal horses almost as much as they loved to count coup on white men.

Slowly advancing, he reached the trees without incident. Every nerve tingling, he entered the cottonwoods. They usually grew near water and these had sprung up around a spring. He came on it shortly and the small fire that crackled nearby. A body lay sprawled facedown. By its size it could only be Garvin Oster.

Two arrows jutted from Oster's broad back.

Saddlebags and their contents as well as several blankets were scattered about.

Fargo read the disaster as surely as if he had been there. Oster and the women had stopped early and made camp. They had been lounging when the Comanches struck. Oster had jumped up and taken the two shafts. The Comanches ransacked their effects and rode off with the women and their horses.

Fargo supposed he should be glad Ginny was still alive. Comanches had little use for white women as it was, and none for older women no warrior would want for a wife.

Climbing down, Fargo sought signs of blood from the struggle. He was relieved there was none other than the blood on the back of Oster's shirt.

Fargo led the Ovaro to the spring and the stallion dipped its muzzle in the water. He figured to let it rest a bit and then push to catch up to the warriors and their captives before nightfall.

Almost as an afterthought, Fargo went to the body. He bent and raised a shoulder high enough to see Oster's face—and Oster opened his eyes. It was so unexpected, Fargo nearly jumped. "Damn," he said.

Oster was in great pain. He had to lick his lips to say, "Ginny and the girl?"

"They took them."

"Both?"

Fargo nodded.

"Thank God." Garvin closed his eyes and clenched his teeth. "I was afraid they'd have killed them."

"I took you for dead."

"Those hostiles must have thought so, too, or they'd have finished me off." Garvin touched his forehead to the ground and his giant frame shook. "I didn't get a good look at them. What tribe, and how many?"

"Comanches, and only four."

"With Comanches four is plenty." Garvin twisted his head to try and see his back. "How many arrows are in me?"

"Two."

"Feels like more," Garvin said. "Dig them out and we'll be on our way."

"We?" Fargo said.

"You'll need my help."

"You're in no shape for a fight."

Garvin looked at him. "They missed my vitals or we wouldn't be havin' this talk. And so long as I'm breathin', nothin' will keep me from savin' those two."

"They took your horse."

"We'll ride double on yours."

"I don't trust you, Oster," Fargo bluntly declared.

"I give you my word that until the women are safe, I won't lift a finger against you."

"I can ride faster without the extra weight."

"Think about it," Garvin said. "Four Comanch and just you, or four Comanch and the two of us."

"No."

"Do I have to beg? That woman is all I care about in this world."

"Ginny Deerforth?"

Oster nodded and confirmed Fargo's suspicion. "She and me are lovers."

30

"I'd hoped I was wrong," Fargo said to himself. To Oster he said, "How long has this been going on?"

"What's it to you?" Oster demanded.

"I'm trying to understand," Fargo said.

With an effort Garvin rose onto an elbow. "I'll tell you all about it after you dig these damn arrows out of me and we're on our way."

"No," Fargo said. "You'll tell me while I dig." Setting down the Henry, he drew the Arkansas toothpick. "I'll have to cut the shirt."

"Do it. Time's a wastin'."

The blood hadn't dried yet so the shirt wasn't stuck fast. One arrow was near the right shoulder blade, the other below the left. Fargo inserted the toothpick's tip and made slits around each. Closer scrutiny revealed that the barbed tips weren't imbedded all that deeply. Oster owed his life to the cords of thick muscle that covered his gigantic frame. "Start talking," Fargo said as he set to work.

Garvin grunted and dug his fingers into the ground. "She and me have been together for years—"

Fargo interrupted with, "She has a husband, or did you forget?"

"Some husband," Garvin spat. "He was hardly ever home. Whole months went by with him away at the capital." He shook slightly, whether from the pain or anger was hard to say.

"She'd have me over for tea on the porch every afternoon. For the longest while all we did was talk. Then I got to likin' her. I got to likin' her a whole lot."

"Ginny Deerforth?"

"Go to hell. She may not be a beauty but she's as good a gal as you'll find anywhere." Garvin paused, and a tone of wonder came into his voice. "She grew to like me, too. Me, who never had any schoolin'. Me, who didn't hardly have a spare dollar to his name. Me, who used to always be a whisker from bein' thrown behind bars."

"True love," Fargo said, working the tip of the toothpick back and forth.

"Keep it up," Garvin growled.

Fargo tried to imagine the two of them together. Ginny, so cultured and urbane and pampered, and Oster, as rough and gruff a specimen as the frontier spawned. "It takes getting used to," he said.

"Not for me it didn't," Garvin said. "She makes me laugh, that gal. Makes me feel mighty fine. And one day back then she invited me into the mansion and, well, one thing led to another and—"

"I don't need to hear that part."

"You asked."

Fargo carefully cut around the barbed tip. It was curved so that if he pulled on the arrow, he'd tear a lot of flesh getting it out. So he didn't try. He cut until the tip was loose enough that he could wriggle it free. "There's one."

"Ginny and me have been lovers since," Garvin resumed. "It ate at me, havin' to sit off in my shack when he came home."

"And you finally couldn't take it anymore," Fargo said, commencing on the second shaft.

"Hell, if it'd been up to her, we'd have run off long ago. She kept sayin' we should. But I couldn't do that to her."

"Do what?"

Garvin twisted his head around. "Don't you see? Ginny is used to livin' high on the hog. She has that fine house and her fancy clothes and servants to wait on her hand and foot. What could I give her?"

Fargo thought he understood. "So you decided to steal the poker stake."

"No, that was her brainstorm. She was sick of bein' with Marion. She said it was high time she severed the tie. Her own words. But she saw we'd need money—a lot of it."

"You think you know people," Fargo said to himself.

"I tried to talk her out of it. I told her we'd have the law after us for the rest of our days. But she had that figured out, too. She said we can go to South America. The law can't touch us there. And a hundred thousand dollars is like a million." Garvin beamed. "Ain't she smart?"

"She's something," Fargo said.

"I figured I could shake a posse. All those years of ridin' the high lines taught me a few things. But you worried me."

"Me?" Fargo said.

"Don't play modest. You're one of the best trackers around. Everyone says so. I knew if you came after us, you'd catch us. So I took steps."

"You hired Ranson and Jules to kill me."

"They were only supposed to cut you bad enough that you couldn't come after us. But when you killed Jules, it made Ranson mad. He wanted you dead for his own self."

"And now you expect me to help you save your sweetheart?"

"And Roselyn," Garvin said. "Don't forget her."

Fargo bent lower. The second tip had gone in deeper and was just below the kidney. He cut with great care.

"What's takin' so long?" Garvin complained.

"I can be reckless if you don't mind bleeding to death."

"Those damned redskins," Garvin said. "That gal is everything to me. If they harm her, I swear—" He didn't finish.

"You're the one brought her into Comanche country."

"I've been through it before," Garvin said, "and didn't lose my scalp."

Fargo had a thought. "If you're going to South America, why didn't you book passage on a ship?"

"Headin' off across the prairie was another of Ginny's brainstorms," Oster answered. "To throw everyone off our scent. We aimed to swing east in a couple of days and head for New Orleans." He grinned. "She thinks of everything, that gal of mine."

"Why drag Roselyn into it?"

"A mother can't leave her daughter behind." Garvin made it sound as if the notion were preposterous.

"So she gets her killed, instead."

"Not if you hurry it up," Garvin said. "Those Comanches made the biggest mistake of their lives."

"Someone has," Fargo said.

31

Fargo's back prickled as if he had a rash. Not from the heat of a Texas summer but from riding double with Garvin Oster. Oster had given his word but it still made him uneasy.

"I'm obliged for this," the big man picked that moment to remark. "I owe you and I won't forget."

"I'm doing it for Roselyn."

"What about Ginny? She's always treated you nice, hasn't she?"

"It's her fault we're in this mess."

"I'm as much to blame as she is," Oster said. "If you have to be mad at somebody, be mad at me."

"I'm curious," Fargo said. "Who kissed who first?"

"What's that got to do with anything?"

"Humor me."

Garvin was quiet awhile and finally cleared his throat. "I had to think on it some but I reckon she kissed me first. But I kissed her right back."

Fargo always thought he was good at reading people. As much wandering as he did and as many cutthroats as he ran into, he had to be. But Ginny Deerforth had hoodwinked him. She put on a great act of being so sweet and devoted to her husband and her family, and all the time she was fooling around behind everyone's back.

"I'd do anything for that gal," Oster went on. "A fine lady like her, carin' for a bumpkin like me. I can't hardly believe it happened."

"Whatever happens, she brought it on her own head," Fargo said. He was more concerned about the girl. "You should have stopped her from bringing Roselyn."

"I couldn't if I wanted to, which I didn't," Garvin said.

"When it comes to some things, Gin-Gin can be as stubborn as a mule."

"Gin-Gin?"

"That's my special name for her. It sort of came out of my mouth one day and she liked it so much, I've used it ever since."

"God, I need a drink."

"What for?"

Fargo didn't answer. He became intent on the trail. The Comanches were heading northwest, toward the heart of their territory. If they reached it, saving the women would be next to impossible.

"You ain't ever cared for someone?" Garvin Oster unexpectedly asked.

"Not to where I'd steal and kill for them." Fargo wished the man would stop jabbering.

"Then you ain't ever been in love. I'm not no great brain with words but I know how I feel and I feel for her like I've never felt for anyone."

Fargo stayed silent, thinking that Oster would take the hint.

"I feel sort of sorry for Marion. It's a terrible thing, stealin' a man's woman out from under him. But if he'd been a better husband this wouldn't have happened."

"Blame him for what you've done," Fargo said. "I like that."

"You have a mouth on you," Garvin said. "You ought not to poke fun at folks like you do. It's not nice."

"You ran off with another man's family," Fargo said. "How nice was that?"

"Damn it," Garvin said. "I'm done talkin'."

Fargo smiled.

On they rode.

Comanches were superb horsemen. In the opinion of some, they were the best. Their mounts were the best, too, and could go for hours without tiring. Fortunately for Fargo, so could the Ovaro. Even bearing double the stallion possessed more stamina than most.

Along about four in the afternoon, Garvin Oster put a hand on Fargo's shoulder and said excitedly, "Do you see what I see?"

Fargo gazed into the distance. "Prairie dogs?"

"Dust," Garvin said, and pointed. "We better go slow. If we can see theirs, they can see ours."

By straining his eyes Fargo could make out what might be faint brown tendrils. "Damn, you have good eyes." He took the advice and reined from a cantor to a walk.

"Always have," Garvin said. "My ma used to say I can see like a hawk." He nudged Fargo. "Do you reckon they'll stop for the night?"

"With the women along, probably."

"That's good. We can sneak on in and give them what for. It's good, too, that Gin-Gin talked me into leavin' you your guns because those red devils took mine."

"You're not to shoot unless I do."

"That's my gal they have. You don't get to tell me what to do."

"Then you don't get a gun."

"I could take one."

Fargo felt Garvin's thick fingers close around the back of his neck.

32

Fargo reacted instantly. He dived from the saddle, drawing as he dropped. The Ovaro came to a halt, and he was in a crouch with the Colt trained on Oster before Oster could think to take the reins. "You son of a bitch."

Garvin looked astounded. He held his hands out from his sides and said, "I was only foolin'. I gave you my word, remember?"

Fargo rose. "Climb down."

"What? Why?"

"From here on out you walk."

"Now see here—" Oster began.

Fargo thumbed back the hammer. "I shoot you, those Comanches are bound to hear. They'll know someone is after them and light a shuck, and you can forget about seeing Gin-Gin ever again."

Garvin's smiled faded. "You've got a lot of bark on you, mister." He lifted his leg over and slid off.

"Move away," Fargo commanded.

Again Garvin complied.

Keeping him covered, Fargo climbed back on the Ovaro. When he had the reins in his hand, he wagged the Colt. "Walk in front of me."

"There's no need to do this, I tell you. I gave you my word." But Garvin did as he was told and set out in the direction they had been going.

Fargo followed.

"I don't much like it when a man won't take me at my word," Garvin persisted.

"I don't much like you hiring two men to carve on me," Fargo said. "I don't much like that you nearly took my head off with that Sharps of yours. I don't much like that you took a fourteen-year-old girl from her home against her will."

"I suppose you don't much like Ginny and me carryin' on behind Marion's back, either."

"I don't judge," Fargo said, especially since he was hardly a paragon of virtue. But he did draw the line at some things.

"You don't realize how lonely she was."

"That's as good an excuse as any."

"What's that mean?"

"People do what they want and then make up excuses for why they do it."

"Gin-Gin and me have been in love for years. That's no excuse. That's how it is."

"I'm tired of talking about this," Fargo said, "so shut the hell up."

Fargo would have thought Comanches had more sense than to let their smoke be seen but he reckoned even Comanches made mistakes now and then. Toward evening, smoke rose from a belt of trees and brush a mile off. He drew rein and announced, "We'll stop here."

"We have a ways to go yet."

"Not until it's dark." Fargo dismounted and stretched. "Have a seat."

"I don't like you bossin' me around."

"Have a seat anyway," Fargo said, and placed his hand on the Colt.

"Damn you." Garvin sank cross-legged, and glared. "This is what I get for sparin' you."

Fargo moved a few yards away and hunkered.

"I have a question," Garvin said. "After we kill those redskins, what then?"

"I turn you over to the marshal."

"That's what I figured. So I'll up my offer. Twenty-five thousand if you'll let Ginny and me ride on."

"Without Roselyn?"

"With her."

"You're wasting your breath."

"Twenty-five thousand is more than most folks see in a lifetime."

"I might have had a hundred thousand if you hadn't sicced those sea dogs on me."

"So that's it. You're still mad on account of them."

"Garvin."

"What?"

"You're a jackass."

Oster tore out a handful of grass and threw it down. "Now you have me mad. I ever get the chance, I aim to wallop you with my bare fists."

The sun crawled down the sky. Fargo saw antelope to the south, and later a pair of hawks flew overhead, searching for prey.

Garvin was sullen and quiet. He glanced often at the distant trees, his worry transparent. Finally he said, "Those savages could be doin' all sorts of things to them."

"We try while it's still light, they'll spot us."

"If they rape her, I'll blame you as much as them."

"Add it to the list."

"I'm startin' not to like you much."

"I'll try not to lose sleep over it," Fargo said.

33

Twilight took forever to shade to night. Stars sparkled and a crescent moon cast a pale gleam over the prairie.

Fargo had been on his feet awhile, pacing, to get his blood flowing. He'd been feeling sluggish and sluggish could get him killed. "We've waited long enough."

"About damn time," Garvin grumbled as he rose and shook himself like a bear roused from hibernation.

"You go ahead of me," Fargo directed.

"I don't get a gun?"

"You don't."

"What am I supposed to fight the Comanches with?"

"Use those big fists of yours."

Swearing, Garvin spat, "When this is over . . ." He didn't elaborate.

Fargo led the Ovaro instead of riding. He left the Henry in the scabbard. In the dark the Colt was just as effective and less unwieldy.

The moonlight both helped and increased the danger. They could see fairly well—and so could the Comanches.

Once they reached the strip of woodland Fargo tied the Ovaro to a tree. Garvin stared at him and then at the saddle scabbard. Fargo shook his head and motioned for him to keep going.

They hadn't taken ten steps when Fargo saw a fire a good fifty yards away. He stopped and whispered for Oster to do the same.

The fire was too big. Indians knew that fires could be seen from a long way off at night, and they never, ever, kindled one that high. Not unless they *wanted* to attract attention.

A small voice inside of his head warned Fargo that they should get out of there, that things weren't as they seemed.

"What are we waitin' for?" Garvin whispered.

"Could be they are luring us in," Fargo said.

"They don't know we're after them."

"Maybe they do," Fargo whispered. "Maybe they knew all along."

"Bah," Garvin said, and continued on. For someone his size, he made no more noise than the breeze.

Fargo's tiny voice screamed at him to get the hell out but he warily trailed after Oster. Stalking from tree to tree, he soon saw two forms curled near the fire. Both wore dresses.

The Comanches weren't there.

Fargo was going to whisper to Oster to stop, that it was indeed a trap, but it was too late.

Out of the darkness rushed four painted forms. Three had lances and the fourth a tomahawk.

Fargo spun. As quick as he was, they were quicker. The blunt end of a lance lashed out and his right hand exploded with pain. His fingers went numb and he dropped the Colt. He retreated, glimpsed Garvin battling two wolfish forms, and then had to focus on his own plight. The other two were on him. He dodged another thrust of the lance. Again, the warrior struck with the blunt end, not the sharp tip. The Comanches wanted to take them alive. Why was easy to guess, and fraught with hideous possibilities.

The other warrior had a tomahawk. Uttering a war whoop, he came in fast and furious, swinging low and then high.

Fargo twisted, ducked. He spun to run and was struck between the shoulder blades so hard, the blow sent him to his knees. He turned. The warrior had thrown the lance, butt end first, and it lay almost within reach. Lunging, he grabbed it as the warrior with the tomahawk launched himself into the air.

Fargo's fingers molded to the shaft and he thrust upward. The Comanche impaled himself. The tip caught him in the middle of his stomach and pierced his body, bursting out his back. He shrieked as he died.

Fargo tried to hold on to the lance but the falling body tore it from his grasp. He reared upright just as the other warrior reached him. The man now held a knife. Fargo had a blade, too; he'd drawn the toothpick as he rose. Steel rang on steel. The Comanche sprang back and circled, seeking an opening. Fargo didn't give him one. They feinted, parried. The warrior was young, Fargo saw. All of them were. Young and eager to count coup and prove themselves to their fellows.

Like a striking adder, the Comanche's knife darted out. Fargo countered, slashed, felt the blade penetrate. The warrior leaped farther back, a dark stain on his wrist. Fargo went after him. He lanced the toothpick high. The tip sheared into the warrior's shoulder but not deep enough to drop him or slow him. Pivoting, the Comanche arced his knife at Fargo's jugular.

Fargo skipped away. The warrior pressed him, stabbing, spearing. Fargo sidestepped, dipped, drove the toothpick at the Comanche's ribs. The blade grated on bone and went in to the hilt.

The warrior stiffened and gasped. He fixed his wide eyes on Fargo and tried to say something. His eyelids fluttered. Fargo yanked the toothpick out and the young warrior pitched to the earth and was still.

Fargo spun, thinking to aid Garvin Oster but Oster didn't need help. The other two Comanches were down and Garvin stood there grinning at him. "We were damned lucky."

Garvin's grinned widened. "I was luckier than you," he said, and brought up his right hand.

He had the Colt.

34

Ten feet separated them. Fargo couldn't reach Garvin before Garvin squeezed the trigger. He didn't try. "Let's see to the women," he said with forced calm.

"Drop your pigsticker."

Fargo stared at the muzzle of his own revolver.

"I hope you try," Oster said. "You didn't kill me so I won't kill you unless you make me."

Fargo let the toothpick fall.

"Damn," Garvin said in disappointment. "Walk to the fire. Arms in the air."

If it wasn't for bad luck, Fargo wryly reflected, he wouldn't have any luck at all. The women hadn't moved; they were blindfolded, bound and gagged.

Beyond were the horses. On the other side of the fire a blanket was bundled on the ground, and poking from under it was the stock to Garvin's Sharps.

Fargo didn't let on that he had seen it.

"That's far enough." Garvin went to the women. "Gin-Gin? Are you all right?"

Ginny Deerforth raised her head and made muffled sounds.

Kneeling, Garvin carefully removed the blindfold and then the wadded piece of buckskin used as a gag. "I'm here," he said. "You're safe now."

Ginny coughed and sputtered. Her eyes glistening, she said, "I thought you were dead. I saw those arrows hit you."

"It takes more than that to kill an ox like me," Garvin said. "Here, let me untie you." Leveling the Colt at Fargo, he moved around behind her. "Don't you try anything."

Ginny said, "He came after us."

"I told you he would," Garvin said.

"Why?" Ginny asked Fargo. "I wrote you that letter explaining everything. I practically begged you."

"If it was just you and him I wouldn't give a damn," Fargo said.

"You want to save Roselyn?"

"She should be with her father."

"I agree," Ginny said.

"You do?"

"It's why I brought her along."

Fargo stared at the still-bound girl and at the woman he once considered a dear friend and lastly at the former foreman of her husband's plantation. "No," he said.

"Yes," Ginny said, smiling. "Roselyn isn't Marion's. She is the fruit of my union with Garvin. I never told Marion nor her, of course, not until right before you caught up to us yesterday. Remember her saying she had something important to tell you?"

"All these years you kept it a secret." Fargo marveled.

"I had to for her sake," Ginny said. "Marion would have disowned her and I couldn't have that. What does it matter if Garvin is her true father? She deserves a share of Marion's wealth, just as I do. Why else did I take the hundred thousand."

"I've lost your trail," Fargo admitted.

"Marion is bound to have his will changed. He'll refuse to leave me a cent even though I stuck with him all these years. As for Roselyn, if he learns the truth he'll disown her. I can't have that. I can't have the two of us penniless and alone."

"You have me," Garvin said.

"Hush, and untie my child." Ginny stood and brushed at her dress. "I'm entitled to some of Marion's money. The hundred thousand is a pittance compared to his true worth but it'll suffice." She muttered something, then said so Fargo could hear, "If the laws in this country were fair, I could ask for a divorce and be given my share of his estate. But only a few states allow divorce. In Texas they are next to impossible to obtain, and then only when the man files the petition. If you're a woman, you're treated like a second-class citizen."

"Marion might have been more reasonable than you think," Fargo remarked. He noticed that Oster had removed Roselyn's gag and was working on her bonds.

"You don't know him like I do. When he is out in public he is warm and friendly and treats everyone as if they are his best friend. That's politics." Ginny paused. "In our marriage, things always had to be done his way. He was the boss and I was his property. His cow. His foot warmer." She shook with the intensity of her vehemence. "I hated that. I hated it with a passion from the moment I learned exactly where I stood. I hated it so much that when another man came along and kindled a spark in my heart, I fanned the flame."

"Garvin Oster."

"Why not?" Ginny challenged. "So what if he's not educated or cultured? He has other qualities that more than make up for his lack of sophistication."

"Name one," Fargo said.

"He has a cock as long as your forearm."

"Mother!" Roselyn exclaimed.

"Gin-Gin," Garvin said, sounding embarrassed.

"Well, you do, and after all those years of Marion and his tiny pickle, I will wear yours out each night."

"I can't believe I'm hearing this," Roselyn said. "What kind of mother are you?"

"The kind who puts her daughter's interests above her own. I stayed with Marion as long as I did because of you. But I can't take it anymore. I want to be happy. I want my own life. I want the man I love."

"Too bad I don't have a fiddle," Fargo said.

Garvin rose and pointed the Colt at him. "What do we do with sassy mouth, here? I say I blow out his wick."

"No," Roselyn said, moving between them. "He's my friend. I won't stand for it."

"Get out of the way, girl."

Roselyn appealed to Ginny. "Don't just stand there, Mother. Tell your lover he's not to shoot, or so help me, I'll hate you for the rest of my life."

"He knows too much," Garvin said.

"Yes, he does," Ginny said. "But we don't want our daughter upset. I propose a compromise."

"What do you have in mind?" Roselyn asked.

Ginny looked at Fargo and her face split in a venomous grin. "Don't worry, my dear. When we leave, your friend here will be in one piece. But he might wish he wasn't." And at that, she laughed.

35

Night had fallen.

For the hundredth time Fargo strained against the ropes that held him to the tree but they barely budged. From his chest to his ankles, there had to be thirty coils. He also had a gag in his mouth, the same wad of buckskin that had been in Ginny's. This was her idea of "compromise": tie him to the tree and leave him to die. Roselyn had protested but it did no good. Garvin Oster tied him and off they went, with the Ovaro and his Colt and the Henry.

This was the last straw, Fargo vowed. If he got out of this fix, he wouldn't go easy on them anymore. From here on, he was out for blood.

Speaking of which, the smell of the pools of blood under several of the dead Comanches was bound to bring every meat eater for a mile around. Fargo suspected that was the whole idea. Let the predators finish him off. He strained again, pushing and trying to kick. The rope was too tight, the knots too secure. He was wasting himself. But he refused to give up. It wasn't in his nature.

Sagging, he rested to recoup his strength. He would keep at it all night and all the next day if he had to.

Keening yips sounded off across the prairie. Coyotes were on the prowl. Normally they didn't worry him. Coyotes were smaller than wolves, and a lot more timid. They rarely attacked people, and when they did, usually it was small children—or someone who was unable to resist.

Fargo looked down at the ropes.

More cries warned him they were closer. Two or three, at least. He heaved at the coils, his sinews bulging, with little effect.

Fargo envisioned how it would be—him defenseless, the coyotes tearing at his legs, their bites bleeding him until he passed out, and then they'd feast. He would hate to die like that. He'd rather go down fighting, or in bed. At the thought, he smiled.

The yips were near the woods. Suddenly they stopped.

Furtive sounds suggested the coyotes were investigating the smells.

Fargo glimpsed eye shine. He had been right. There were three of them. He heard them sniff. They circled, their natural wariness keeping them at bay, but it wouldn't hold them off for long.

A pair of eyes fixed on him. Out of the murk stalked a male.

Fargo yelled and struggled and the coyote wheeled and ran. It went only a dozen feet and stopped. Looking back, it realized he wasn't in pursuit. It stalked him a second time and again he yelled and thrashed and again it ran off, but not as far.

The other coyotes watched.

Fargo surged, tugged, furiously worked his arms and legs. The ropes held fast.

And the coyote came back.

Once more Fargo shouted but now the coyote didn't run. It growled. It had sensed he wasn't a threat. The others continued to watch as the male sank low to the ground. He hollered and moved his feet. He swore. He roared. He went into a frenzy of struggling to break free.

The coyote slunk up to him and growled.

Fury boiled Fargo's blood. To die like *this*. He tried to kick the coyote. It snarled and lunged and bit. Expecting to feel pain, Fargo was surprised when there wasn't any. He glanced down. The coyote's teeth had torn into the rope, not into him. He couldn't be sure, but it looked as if the rope was partially severed. He looked at the coyote and smiled. "Do that again, you mangy son of a bitch."

The coyote bared its fangs and attacked.

This time Fargo felt it. Teeth sank into his legs. They also sank into the rope. Six or seven times the coyote slashed and snapped. Then it bounded back.

Fargo tilted his head. His left leg had been bitten below the knee. His pants were torn but no blood showed. He bent further, and hope swelled. The bottommost coil hung by a shred. He kicked some more, one foot and then the other, and whooped when the coil broke and the two ends fell. He kicked harder, putting all his leg muscles into it, and felt the rope slacken.

The coyote slunk in for another try, and stopped. All his movement was giving it pause.

Fargo went on kicking and struggling. One by one, the loops came loose and dropped away. He was free from the hips down when the coyote marshaled its courage and sprang. He caught it in midleap with his boot and sent it tumbling. In a twinkling it scrambled upright.

Fargo struggled harder. Suddenly his hands were free. He pried and yanked. Now there was only the coil around his neck and the knots that held it in place. Quickly, he gripped the rope and slid it around so he could get at the knots.

The coyote, tenacious, came for him anew.

Fargo undid one of the knots. Out of the corner of his eye he saw a second coyote creeping toward him. He dug his nails into the hemp.

The coyotes glanced at one another. As if that were a signal, they both crouched and sprang.

36

Fargo swung his right boot and sent the nearest coyote tumbling. He kicked at the other but it danced away.

The last knot was coming undone but not fast enough. He pried, wrenched and was free. He threw the rope at them and ran to the fallen Comanches. A third coyote streaked out of nowhere and nipped at his hamstring. Jumping straight up, he slammed his boots down on top of it. The coyote yelped and scrabbled to safety.

A lance lay near an outstretched hand. Grabbing it, Fargo wheeled just as the first male rushed him. He met it with the tip, spearing into its chest with all the force in his shoulders and arms. Its death rattle was ghastly. Ripping the lance out, he spun to confront the other two but they'd had enough and were flying for their lives.

Fargo straightened and waited. When he was sure they were gone, he found his toothpick and slid it into his ankle sheath. He also picked up a tomahawk.

He debated going after Ginny and Oster and dismissed the idea as futile. They had too much of a head start, and they had horses.

All that night he jogged to the southeast. Tireless as an Apache, he covered mile after mile. Now and again he stopped briefly to rest.

Several times growls and grunts warned him predators were near but they left him alone.

Dawn broke, and Fargo climbed a low hill, curled on his side in the grass, and slept soundly for several hours. Then he was up and jogging again.

A cramp slowed him but it went away. As the sun climbed he began to sweat. Soon his buckskins clung to him like a second skin. He passed a prairie dog town and they whistled in alarm. He went around a rattler that slithered into his path. Later he startled a rabbit and wished he had his rifle. The thought of food made his stomach growl.

Fargo hoped that Marshal Moleen hadn't turned back. If so, Ginny and Oster would get clean away.

Toward the middle of the afternoon he spied a small brown cloud to the south. He changed direction and within half an hour could make out the riders raising the dust. He stopped to wait for them. When the lead rider raised an arm, he returned the gesture.

The posse slowed from a trot to a walk and drew rein. Surprise was on every face.

Moleen leaned on his saddle horn and said, "Lose something?"

"Where's your horse?" Lacey Mayhare asked.

"In a minute," Fargo said. He went up to Vin Creed's mount and tapped Creed's canteen. "I could use a drink."

"Traded your pistol and rifle for a spear and a tomahawk, did you?" the gambler said as he handed it down.

Fargo opened the canteen and thirstily gulped. He poured some into his palm and wet his throat and his brow.

"You were jumped by hostiles, is that it?" Senator Deerforth said.

"My word," Benton exclaimed. The banker's cheeks were red from the sun and he had unbuttoned the top three buttons of his shirt. "Is that a bite mark on your leg?"

Marshal Moleen shifted. "We might as well climb down, folks."

Fargo capped the canteen and gave it back to Creed. "I'm obliged." The senator, the banker and Lacey all asked questions at once and he held up a hand. "Here's what happened," he began, and gave a brief recital. He didn't mention that Ginny and Oster had been secret lovers for years, or that Roselyn was the result of their affair, or that it was Ginny's idea to steal the one hundred thousand. He said only that he'd caught up to them, been taken by surprise, and left weaponless to fend for himself. He ended with, "I'd like to borrow three horses and head out after them."

"That would strand three of us afoot," Benton said.

"The marshal and his deputies will look after you."

"I think I know what you aim to do," Marshal Moleen said.

"I wish someone would explain it to me," Lacey said.

"I'll ride in relays." Fargo enlightened her. "When one horse tires I'll switch to another." He could cover three times as much ground in half the time.

"You figure to stop Oster with a spear?" Vin Creed said skeptically.

"I'll need to borrow a gun, too."

"You're asking for a hell of a lot," banker Benton declared.

"Do you want the money back or not?"

"I do," Senator Deerforth said, "but I want my wife and my daughter back even more. Take whatever you need. We'll stay here until you return."

Benton looked at each of the others and said, "But what if he doesn't?"

"Thanks for the confidence," Fargo said.

37

Fargo was tired. He'd been riding for hours and night was approaching. He was on the senator's chestnut. Trailing after it, secure to a lead rope, were the two animals the deputies had been riding. He hadn't used them yet. In the morning he would. He would push like hell and with luck overtake Oster and Ginny before the day was out. For now, he sought a spot to camp.

A basin rich with grass was as good a haven as any. He stripped the horses and was under a blanket by the time stars filled the firmament. He didn't make a fire. Where there were four Comanches there may be more.

Fargo lay propped on his saddle with the revolver he had borrowed in his hand. He wondered if he had done the right thing in sparing Deerforth the truth. It was bound to come out when he returned with Ginny and the girl.

The prairie was quiet and sleep soon claimed him. His rest was undisturbed. At the crack of the new day he was up and getting ready, and when a golden crown blazed the east, he was under way. He switched horses every hour, his mounts eating the miles so rapidly that before noon he looked down at the dead Comanches.

The coyotes had been at the bodies and they were grisly ruins.

Fargo didn't stop. The sign was plain enough, and he smiled grimly when he saw that his quarry had held to a walk.

Oster and Ginny must have thought he was as good as dead and they had no need to hurry.

He switched to the senator's chestnut. It had an easy gait and a fair amount of stamina.

Late in the afternoon the tracks told him he was close.

When the prairie gave way to a long, winding valley, he drew rein on a ridge that overlooked it and scanned the timber that framed the bottomland. He didn't see them but he was sure they were down there somewhere.

Fargo descended to the valley floor. The chestnut raised its head and sniffed. Water was near and the horse knew it.

He hugged cover until he came to a slow-flowing creek. At a shallow pool he drew rein and let the horses drink. When they had enough he took them into the trees and tied them.

The sun was sinking when Fargo climbed a high oak. From his vantage he could scan the valley from end to end. It wasn't long before a flickering orange finger a quarter of a mile away brought a grim smile.

Climbing down, Fargo drew the short-barreled Remington Vin Creed had lent him. The front sight had been filed down and the trigger guard removed. It held five cartridges in the cylinder, not six like his Colt.

Fargo removed his spurs and stuck them in the chestnut's saddlebags. He left the horses and glided along the creek until the glow reappeared. With consummate care he crept forward.

Garvin Oster and Ginny were seated side by side. Across from them was Roselyn, glumly poking the ground with a stick. Their horses and the Comanches' horses and the Ovaro were tied in a string.

Sinking flat, Fargo crawled. He saw that Oster had the Henry across his lap.

Roselyn was jabbing that stick fit to break it. The angry glances she cast at her mother and Oster explained why.

"Will you stop that?" Ginny said.

"No."

"It annoys me."

"I don't care."

Garvin stirred and said, "You'll do as your mother tells you, girl."

"Or what? You'll take me over your knee?"

"You're not too old for a spankin'," Garvin said.

Roselyn pointed the stick at him. "You ever so much as lay a finger on me, I'll scratch your eyes out."

"That will be enough of that kind of talk," Ginny said. "I want us to get along."

"Let me go back," Roselyn said.

"Not again," Ginny said, and sighed. "How many times have we been through this? There is no going back, not now, not ever. You're my daughter and you're with me from here on out."

"I don't want to be with you. I want to be with my father."

"You are."

Roselyn glowered at Garvin Oster. "Did he raise me? No. Did he show me the love a father should? No. Calling him that doesn't make it so."

"Consarn you, girl," Garvin said. "I would if I could have but your ma said we had to be careful."

"I've always done what I thought best for you," Ginny said.

"You wouldn't know what is best if it bit you on the ass, Mother."

"Roselyn!"

"Don't talk to your ma like that," Garvin warned.

"I hate you," Roselyn said. "I hate the both of you for what you've done to my life. I hate you for taking me against my will, and the secret you've hid all these years. I hate you and I wish you were dead."

"You don't mean that," Ginny said.

Roselyn uttered a cry of exasperation. "If I had a gun I swear I would shoot you both."

Ginny smiled lovingly. "You don't have it in your heart to kill us."

Fargo rose and strode into the circle of firelight. "I do."

38

To Garvin Oster's credit, he didn't try to use the Henry. All he did was blink and say, "I'll be damned."

Ginny started to jump up but caught herself and muttered, "He has more lives than a cat."

Roselyn leaped to her feet. "Skye!" she cried, and would have flung herself into Fargo's arms had he not motioned for her to stay where she was.

"First things first," Fargo said. He moved around behind Oster and Ginny and pressed the Remington's muzzle to the back of Garvin's head. "Slide my rifle behind you."

"Anything to please," Garvin said. Gripping the Henry by the barrel, he complied.

"Where's my Colt?"

"In your saddlebags. I didn't have any use for it."

"Fetch it for me," Fargo said to Roselyn, and the girl flew to the horses. He went around to the other side of the fire.

Garvin seemed puzzled by something. "Why am I still breathin'? Were I in your boots, I'd have put a slug in my skull."

"I thought about it," Fargo said. "But I owe it to Marion to take you back alive."

Ginny looked over her shoulder. "Where is he?" she apprehensively asked.

"Waiting for me to get back with the horses I borrowed."

"So that's how you caught us," Garvin said.

"Wait." Ginny went rigid. "You've seen them since we saw you last?" She paled. "You told Marion about Garvin and me, didn't you?"

"I'm leaving that for you," Fargo said.

"Oh, God."

Garvin touched her arm. "Why are you upset? Your husband would have figured it for himself sooner or later."

"Maybe not," Ginny said.

"I don't savvy," Garvin said.

Roselyn returned bearing the Colt. She handed it to Fargo and said, "I flatter myself that I understand. I'm beginning to learn how my mother thinks."

"You hush," Ginny said.

Roselyn stared at Garvin. "So long as my father doesn't learn the truth, she can go back to him if things go wrong."

"She wouldn't do that," Garvin said.

"Think about it," Roselyn said. "As far as he knows, you stole the money and you stole us. He doesn't know about you and her. He doesn't know that it was her idea to steal the money. That it was her who came up with the plan to run away to South America. It's all on your head."

"But you and Fargo know."

"She thought Skye was dead and she kept me with her so I couldn't tell anyone."

Garvin turned to Ginny. "Tell me she's got it wrong. Tell me you wouldn't toss me over in a minute if it would save your hide."

"Of course I wouldn't. The child is trying to create a rift between us. Any fool could see that."

"So I'm a fool now, am I?"

Ginny patted his cheek "You know how much I adore you. I was just hoping to spare Marion's feelings."

"I don't know as I believe you, Gin-Gin."

"Enough." Fargo wasn't about to let them get into another of their long-winded arguments. He had Roselyn bring a rope and asked her to tie their hands behind their backs.

"With pleasure."

"You wouldn't!" Ginny said as her daughter moved behind her.

"Watch me."

The girl took so much delight in it, Fargo grinned. He instructed her to tie their legs, too.

The pot of coffee they'd made—using his pot—was three-fourths full. Fargo filled a cup, blew on the steaming coffee, and sat. "In the morning we'll head back."

"What will happen to them?" Roselyn asked, joining him.

Fargo shrugged. "Oster might end up swinging from a rope. Your mother will likely spend a few years behind bars."

"I hope it's more than a few," Roselyn said.

"Listen to you," Ginny said sorrowfully. "To talk about your own mother like that, as if all the years I've devoted to you mean nothing."

A gust of wind fanned the fire. Fargo raised his head and caught the scent of moisture.

"Marion would never let them put me in prison," Ginny boasted. "He cares for me too much."

"You slept with another man, Mother," Roselyn said. "Not once but over a period of years. And now you've deserted the man you were married to to be with your lover. Father will wash his hands of you, and I say good riddance."

"My own daughter," Ginny said.

"Stop saying that."

Another gust bent the trees. From off to the west came a low rumble.

"Was that thunder?" Roselyn asked.

"A storm is coming," Fargo said. At that time of the year it wasn't uncommon for thunderheads to sweep across the prairie at any hour of the day or night.

"Are we in any danger?"

Fargo wanted to say no but that would be a lie.

39

It was almost midnight when nature unleashed the tempest.

By then Fargo had made sure the horses were securely tied and toted the saddlebags and saddles under a pine and covered them. It was the best he could do. There was no shelter to be had and trying to outrun the storm was pointless.

At first a few cold drops fell. The shrieking wind whipped the trees and the rain became stinging barbs. Then, with a blast that shook the ground and a bolt that lit half the valley, the storm was on them.

Almost immediately the fire was extinguished. It hissed and gave off smoke that the wind swept away before it could rise.

Huddled with a blanket over his head and shoulders, Fargo watched the woods churn into a frenzy. He'd thought about moving from the clearing into the trees. They'd have better cover but the risk from lightning was greater, and they'd end up just as wet.

Another bolt splashed pale light. To his right, a blanket over her head, was Roselyn. Ginny and Garvin were on their sides. He'd covered them with blankets, and Garvin's was flapping as if to be airborne.

The Henry was in Fargo's lap, the Colt in his holster.

He figured he had the situation under control. The storm would pass and they'd rekindle the fire and in the morning they would be on their way.

The cannonade of thunder was near continuous. The same with the vivid streaks that produced it. Nearby bolts illuminated the clearing. Distant ones didn't. One minute they were in bright light, the next mired in black pitch. It went on like that for half an hour. Gradually the lightning diminished and they were in the dark for longer periods.

"How much more of this?" Roselyn asked. She sounded miserable.

"It's almost over," Fargo assured her. The wind had lessened from banshee wails to mewling like a neglected infant.

Fargo peered out from under his hat brim, as anxious as she was for it to be over but for a different reason. He didn't mind the wet so much. He was used to it.

A celestial spear cleaved the sky, lighting up them and the clearing.

Fargo clearly saw Roselyn with her head under the blanket, and Ginny huddled against the chill—and an empty spot where Garvin Oster had been. In a twinkling he was on his feet, the blanket discarded. He spun to the right and the left but there was no sign of him. Cursing, he wrapped an arm around Roselyn, bodily lifted her, and was in among the trees in a few bounds.

"What in the world?" Roselyn's head poked out. "What are you doing?"

"Hush," Fargo cautioned. "Oster is loose."

"Oh my God."

Fargo pushed her down and crouched. Oster wouldn't be taken alive if he could help it; he'd want horses and guns, and Ginny.

"What do we do?"

"I said to hush up."

"Sorry."

Fargo pivoted on his heels, turning in a slow circle. Rain still fell but not heavily. The trees weren't bending as fiercely. But the sounds were loud enough that he wouldn't hear Oster until Oster was on top of him.

"What about my mother?"

The girl just wouldn't listen.

A bolt struck a good ways off, the glow faint but enough that Fargo could see Ginny where they had left her.

A whinny brought him around with the Henry to his shoulder. He caught movement at the end of the horse string. "Stay here," he commanded. In the dark the animals were vague shapes. He crept down the line, counting them.

One was missing.

Fargo scowled. He stalked to the other side. The woods

were a patchwork of black and almost black, impossible to penetrate. To go in after Oster would be folly.

He suspected that Oster would try to take another horse but the minutes dragged and no attempt was made. The rain ended and all was quiet save for the drops dripping from the trees.

Fargo wondered if he was making a mistake. Oster might go for Ginny, instead. He glided over.

The drenched blanket was over her shoulders and she was shivering badly. "Get the fire going, will you?" she pleaded. "I'm freezing."

"In a minute." Fargo turned to where he had left the daughter. "Roselyn?"

The girl was gone.

40

"I don't understand it," Ginny Deerforth said for the tenth or eleventh time since they set out. "I don't understand how he can abandon me."

Fargo was tired of hearing her gripe.

"I thought he cared for me," Ginny said. "I thought he loved me. Yet he takes her and goes off and leaves me to my fate."

Fargo scanned the prairie. He was leading the horses save for the one Ginny was on. They had been riding most of the day.

"Does he care for her more than he does for me? Is that what this means?"

Butterflies flitted about a patch of blue wildflowers.

"I asked you a question," Ginny said.

"He's your lover."

"Must you be so callous?" Ginny indignantly demanded. "You could at least be glad for my sake that I found love and happiness."

Fargo sighed and shook his head. "Ginny, I thought I knew you. I was wrong. You're not a sweet old lady. You're a conniving bitch."

"We've known each other how many years and you can say that to me?"

"A lot of women would give anything to be in your shoes. You had everything and you threw it away."

"Everything?" Ginny said, her color up. "Oh, yes, I had a powerful and wealthy husband who treated me the same as he does his gold watch. I'm something to be put on display when the occasion warrants. Otherwise, I'm to mind my manners and never interfere and suffer in silence the many weeks and months that he's being important and I'm left all alone."

"No marriage is perfect, or so I hear tell."

"Quit defending him. God knows I bore it as long as I could. I did all sorts of things to keep busy. I sewed. I took up knitting. But part of me was always miserable, and terribly lonely."

"So you took up with dumb as a stump."

"Garvin is *not* dumb. He's rustic and rough around the edges but he can be ruthlessly intelligent when he has to be. If not for me, he'd have killed you by now."

"I aim to repay the favor."

"Why didn't you when you had the chance? You had the drop on us. You could easily have shot him."

"I don't gun people down in cold blood."

"But if he'd resisted, if he'd gone for his gun, you would have blown him away and not given it a second thought. Is that how it is?"

"That's exactly how it is. Now shut the hell up."

To Fargo's relief, she did. The miles fell behind them. Evening was on the cusp of descending when he spied a point of light on the southern horizon and allowed himself a smile. "Another hour or so," he announced.

Ginny raised her head, and trembled. "Must you do this? Why not simply let me go?"

"You're forgetting Roselyn."

"I'm forgetting nothing. She's my daughter. I have every right to have her with me."

"Except she doesn't want to be."

"I know best," Ginny declared. "She's a snip of a girl with little experience. I'll look after her, protect her. Trust me when I say she'll have the best life I can provide."

"In South America."

"What does it matter where so long as she has loving parents? Garvin will be a better father than Marion could ever hope to be."

"I've seen how the senator treats her. He's a damn good father."

"Only because he doesn't know she isn't his. Which reminds me. You told me that you didn't tell him. Why not? To spare his feelings?"

"I figured I'd leave that for you."

"He'll throttle me. Or have me thrown behind bars. Either way, my life is over."

"You'll get what you deserve."

"I *deserve* to be happy. That's not too much to ask out of life, is it? Garvin makes me happy in ways Marion never could."

"I bet he's a bull in bed."

"Goodness, you can be crude. Our intimate moments are none of your business. I'll thank you not to bring them up."

"The last thing I want to think about," Fargo assured her, "is you naked."

"You, sir, are a pig."

"One of us is," Fargo said.

The drum of hooves brought the posse to its feet with weapons in their hands. Fargo hailed them and rode into the circle of firelight and drew rein.

"Ginny!" Senator Deerforth exclaimed, and ran up. He dropped his rifle and reached for her, and turned to stone. "Why in the world are your hands tied?"

"She has something to tell you," Fargo said.

Ginny glared at him. "I hate you."

"I'll try not to lose sleep over it."

"What's going on?" the senator asked in confusion. He helped her down and put his hand on her wrists. "Dearest, I'll have you free in a moment."

"No," Fargo said, dismounting. "You won't." To Ginny he said, "Get on with it."

Slowly, haltingly, Ginny Deerforth related her years of dalliance with the foreman, and the result of their secret union.

Everyone listened in silence. The senator and the banker were stunned. Lacey Mayhare kept snorting and shaking her head as if she thought Ginny was loco. Vin Creed sipped his flask and grinned.

Marshal Moleen grew somber. When Ginny finished and bowed her head, he was the first to speak. "So Oster still has the girl and neither of you have any notion where they got to?"

Fargo nodded.

"I'm afraid I don't," Ginny said.

"We'll head out after them at first light," Moleen told Fargo.

"The rain washed out their trail," Fargo mentioned. Or he would have gone after them himself.

"We can't give up," the lawman said. "I like that girl. She's sweet as can be."

"Wait," Lacey said. "What I want to know is where's my money?"

"Imagine that," Vin Creed said, and laughed.

"Ginny has it," Fargo said, "in a money belt around her waist."

Ginny glanced up. "How did you know?"

Fargo knew she wouldn't entrust it to Garvin and it hadn't been in her saddlebags or hidden in her bedroll. And besides that—"It shows when you bend over."

"Forget the damn money," Senator Deerforth said. "How do we go about getting my daughter back?"

"Didn't you hear me?" Ginny said. "She's not yours."

Deerforth turned. "I've raised her. I've clothed her, fed her, sat with her when she was sick. I've been a father to her. Not your precious lover." He rubbed his eyes and said sadly, "I could forgive you for stealing the prize money, Virginia. I could even forgive you for taking up with Garvin. But I'll never forgive you for what you've put poor Roselyn through."

"You needn't worry," Ginny said. "Wherever Garvin is, I'm sure she's perfectly safe."

Just then a deep voice bellowed out of the night, "I'm right here! And unless you do as I say, so help me, I'll snap the girl's neck."

41

In the shocked silence that followed, they all heard muffled sounds, as of someone trying to speak or yell through a gag. And they could tell who it was: Roselyn.

"Garvin?" Ginny shouted. "What on earth are you doing?"

Marshal Moleen motioned for her to be quiet and stepped past them, his rifle raised. "Garvin!" he hollered. "Use your head. Come in with your hands up. I promise no harm will come to you."

"Until I'm hung," Garvin shouted.

"The judge won't send you to the gallows for robbery," Marshal Moleen said, "but he will for murder. Let the girl go and surrender."

"So long as I have her, you won't lift a finger against me."

"We know she's your daughter."

"And you know me, Floyd," Oster said. "I'll do what I have to."

"Oh, Garvin," Ginny said.

Oster raised his voice. "Here is how it'll be. Send Ginny out with her horse and mine. She's to bring my rifle and my six-gun plus a canteen and food. We'll leave you be, and you're not to follow us."

"I can't do that," Marshal Moleen said.

"You can and you will."

Senator Deerforth was peering into the darkness. "Garvin, please. I'm begging you. Let my daughter go."

"She's not yours, Marion. She's mine. But I'll tell you what. She doesn't want anything to do with me. So I give you my word, the first town we come to, I'll let her go."

Marshal Moleen interjected, "That's not good enough. We can't let you take her."

"You can't stop me, Floyd."

"Stop calling me that."

Deerforth gripped the lawman's arm. "Listen to me. I don't care about the money." He glanced at his wife. "I don't care about Ginny. All I want is my daughter back, safe. Give him what he wants."

Marshal Moleen shrugged loose. "Damn it, Marion. I'm wearing the badge here."

"It's *Roselyn* we're talking about."

Moleen swore, then jerked his rifle down. "Oster? I'll make a deal. Give the girl to us and you can have Mrs. Deerforth and the horses and the guns. I'll give you until dawn before I come after you. That's the best I can do."

"And the money?" Garvin yelled.

"You can have that, too."

"Like hell he can," Lacey Mayhare said.

"Stay out of this," Ginny snapped. "It doesn't concern you."

"Like hell it doesn't." Lacey stepped over to her. "Those are my winnings. Hand over the money belt and be quick about it, bitch."

"How dare you," Ginny said, and backhanded Lacey across the cheek with her bound hands.

Lacey shot her. She raised a pocket pistol and pointed it at Ginny's face and fired. It knocked Ginny back, the slug smashing her nose and coring her head to burst out the back of her skull. Ginny's eyes widened and her mouth moved but it was reflex; she was dead on her feet.

Fargo reached them first. He tore the pistol from Lacey's grasp and she spun on him and clawed at his face.

"Give that back to me!"

"Damn it." Marshal Moleen lunged and seized her arms. Holding her fast, he bellowed at his deputies to take her from him.

"Oh, God!" the banker bleated, staring aghast at Ginny.

"Virginia?" Senator Deerforth said, holding out his hand to her as her lifeless husk melted to the ground.

"Didn't see that coming," Vin Creed said, and tipped his flask.

Moleen dropped to one knee and pressed his fingers to Ginny Deerforth's throat.

"What in God's name are you doing, Marshal?" Creed asked. "Her brains are splattered all over my pants. They don't get any deader than that."

Moleen rose and glowered at Lacey Mayhare. "What have you done?"

Lacey was struggling to break free of the deputies. "You heard her. I wasn't about to let her steal my winnings."

"You killed the woman in cold blood," Marshal Moleen rasped.

"She attacked me," Lacey said. "All of you saw it. All I did was defend myself."

"You murdered her," Moleen said. "And I'll see to it that you are charged and brought to trial."

"Go ahead," Lacey taunted. "No jury would convict me for protecting what's mine."

The marshal balled his fists.

"Moleen," Fargo said quietly.

"Eh?" Moleen said, his whole attention on Lacey.

"Oster," Fargo said.

The lawman straightened and turned and said half under his breath, "God." He cupped a hand to his mouth. "Garvin? You saw what happened. We can still make a deal for the girl. You can still have the money belt."

"No, he can't," Lacey said.

"Garvin?" Moleen yelled louder. "Are you still out there? Talk to me?"

There was no answer.

42

Fargo and the lawman took torches and searched. Moleen hollered until he was nearly hoarse.

"He took her. That poor girl. There's no telling what he'll do." Moleen kicked a clump of grass. "Damn Lacey, anyhow. If Roselyn dies on account of her, I hope she rots in prison for the rest of her life."

"Garvin might have other ideas."

The lawman scratched his chin. "I hadn't thought of that but it would serve her right." He swore bitterly. "Who am I kidding? I have to protect her the same as I would anyone."

"It must be hell sometimes, wearing that badge," Fargo said.

"Mister, you don't know the half of it."

They went back.

Senator Deerforth was on his knees beside his wife, clasping her hand, tears trickling down his cheeks. Benton was behind him, a hand on his shoulder. The deputies still had hold of Lacey, who had stopped resisting. Vin Creed was drinking.

"Tell them to let me go," Lacey demanded, tugging. "You can't treat me like this."

"Like hell we can't. You're under arrest," Marshal Moleen informed her. He gestured. "Tie her, boys, hand and feet."

Fargo waited until they were done and had gone to the fire. He sat, crossed his legs, and placed his elbows on his knees. "Fine mess you're in."

"She had it coming," Lacey said.

"That won't help you much in court."

"I'll bat my eyes and show some cleavage and throw myself on the mercy of the judge," Lacey said.

"It won't work if he has scruples."

"I'm not worried. I'll send for the best lawyer in Texas. I can afford it."

"That's what I want to talk to you about. Your money."

"What about it?"

"I aim to trade it to Oster for Roselyn."

Lacey cocked her head. "Are you loco? If you give it to him I'll never see it again."

"There's the girl to think of."

"You think of her. She's nothing to me. I feel sorry for her having that bitch for a mother but I'm not going to shed any tears."

"I'd take it as a favor."

Lacey snorted. "You make it sound as if I owe you. I don't. We had fun in bed once. That's it."

"The thing is," Fargo said, "you killing Ginny might send Oster over the edge. She kept him from killing me, and doing worse. Now that she's gone—" He shrugged.

"All I'm interested in is my money, and no, you can't have it."

Fargo stood and adjusted his gun belt. Stepping to the fire, he held his palms to the flames. "I'm going after Oster and the girl in the morning."

"You already told me," Marshal Moleen reminded him.

"I'm saying it again because I'm taking the money belt."

The lawman was about to pour coffee. He stopped, the cup in one hand, the pot in the other. "That's not your decision to make."

"I give him the money belt, he gives us the girl," Fargo said.

"Or you keep it for yourself," a deputy said.

Marshal Moleen shook his head. "No. I'm sorry. I can't allow that."

"You don't have a say," Fargo said, and drew his Colt.

The deputies stiffened but the lawman calmly poured his coffee.

"You won't shoot us. Not in cold blood."

"True," Fargo said. "But if you draw on me, I will. And I'm taking that belt."

"Do you really think Garvin will agree to a trade?"

"I have to try."

Moleen held the cup in both hands. "Is it that she's a girl or fourteen or what?"

"She was nice to me."

"That's all it takes?" Moleen grinned. "Hell. You're welcome to it, and be sure to bring it back when you're done."

"You have my word." Fargo backed to where the senator knelt next to Ginny. "You heard?"

"Yes."

"Get it off her."

"In front of everyone?"

"She's dead. She won't hardly care."

Benton the banker was twitching as if he was about to throw a fit. "Well, *I* care. I don't know as we can trust you any more than we could Mr. Oster."

"I agree," Lacey said, attempting to sit up. "That's my money, damn you."

"So you keep telling us."

"If I wasn't hog-tied I'd shoot you."

Vin Creed chuckled. "I should thank all you folks. This is more entertaining than the Orpheum Theater."

"You're so drunk, you don't know what's going on," Lacey said scornfully.

"On the contrary, madam," Creed responded. "I can drink all day and half the night and not be affected." He paused. "I always know exactly what I am about."

Deerforth, with great reluctance, was unfastening his wife's buttons. "I'm sorry, dearest," he said to the corpse. "It has to be done."

"No, it doesn't," Benton said. "I am strongly against this, Marion. What do we know about this man other than his reputation for gambling and womanizing?"

"Fargo likes women?" Creed said, and cackled.

"You're despicable, sir," Benton said.

"At least I'm not a tub of lard."

Benton grew red. His twitching became worse. "I simply cannot permit this." With that, he spun toward Fargo, swept his jacket aside, and grabbed for his revolver.

43

Fargo had expected him to try something. He took two strides and slammed his Colt against the banker's temple and Benton staggered. Relieving him of the six-shooter, Fargo tripped him and Benton fell onto his backside. "Stay there," Fargo said.

Vin Creed clapped his hands. "Well done. While you're standing there, why don't you kick Lacey in the teeth?"

"Go to hell, Creed," Lacey said. "What did I ever do to you?"

"You won the money I wanted."

Benton groaned and put a hand to his temple. "You hit me, damn you."

"I'll do it again if you try to get up," Fargo warned.

The banker looked at the marshal. "Are you just going to sit there? Arrest him for assaulting me."

"You went for your gun," Moleen said. "You brought it on yourself."

"Marion?" Benton appealed to the senator. "Say something. Do something. I've been hurt. Demand that our marshal be true to his oath of office."

"I'll say something," Deerforth said, continuing to undo buttons and stays. "Shut up, Stanley. You're making a nuisance of yourself."

"I'm trying to protect your interests."

"The money is no longer mine. My only interests, as you call them, were my wife and my daughter. My wife is gone, and I'll be damned if I'll let my daughter share her fate. So shut the hell up and let Fargo try to save her. He's her only hope."

"I never," Benton said.

"As old as you are?" Creed said. "There's a whorehouse

over to Dallas you should visit. The ladies there will curl your toes."

"Why would I want to bed a whore?" Benton asked.

Lacey hadn't taken her eyes off of Fargo. "Listen to me, you bastard. If you don't bring my money back, I'll hunt you down. I'll find you and I'll do to you what I did to that stupid cow."

Senator Deerforth looked up, scowling. "I'll thank you not to insult my wife."

"It's her fault we're here," Lacey said. "She was the one who slept with your foreman. She was the one who had the idea to steal my winnings. This is all her doing."

"Maybe so," Deerforth said, "but I won't have her name besmirched."

"It already is, you jackass."

"The money belt," Fargo prompted.

Deerforth nodded and finished undoing the dress. Parting it just enough that he could see under but no one else could, he slipped his hand inside. In a minute he fumbled the money belt free. "Here you go."

Fargo had seen money belts before. He'd worn one, once, years ago, when he'd been hired to carry an army payroll to a remote outpost. He'd never seen one like this. For one thing, it was made of soft cotton and not leather. For another, it was pink.

"I can't wait to see you put it on," Vin Creed said.

"All that money," Benton lamented.

Fargo twirled the Colt into his holster. Hiking his shirt, he wrapped the money belt around his waist. It overlapped by a good foot and a half.

"That gal sure had a belly on her," Creed remarked.

"Please show some respect for the dead," Deerforth scolded him.

"Sorry, Senator. Sometimes my mouth gets ahead of my head."

By twisting the extra around the belt, Fargo fit it snugly enough that it wouldn't come off. He lowered his buckskin shirt and patted the bulge.

"Better go on a diet," Vin Creed said.

"Will someone please shut him up?" Benton requested.

Marshal Moleen cleared his throat. "We should all turn in. I'm planning to get an early start back to town."

"Wouldn't it be wiser to remain here until Skye returns with my daughter?" Deerforth asked.

"There's no telling how long it will take him," Marshal Moleen said. "And with a prisoner, and Comanches about, we're asking for trouble if we stay much longer."

"I don't feel right about leaving," Deerforth said. "Roselyn will think I've deserted her."

"I'll tell her how it is," Fargo promised. "She's a smart kid. She'll understand."

"It's settled then," Marshal Moleen said. "In about fifteen minutes I'm putting out the fire. Anyone wants to stay up, they do it in the dark."

Lacey Mayhare shook her bound wrist at him. "What about me? How can I sleep trussed up?"

"It's real easy," the lawman said. "You close your eyes."

Lacey switched her anger to Fargo. "And you. Nothing better happen to my winnings, you hear? When and if you rescue that kid, bring the money straightaway to me."

"And here I was looking forward to a wild spree in Saint Louis."

"Men," Lacey snarled. "You're all a bunch of bastards."

"I'll drink to that," Vin Creed said.

44

Fargo couldn't say what woke him. Without raising his head he checked the other sleepers. In the pale starlight they were mounds of blankets and bodies. To his left were the senator and the banker. Creed was next. To his right were the marshal and one of the deputies. The third deputy was supposed to be keeping watch. Moleen had told them to take turns and Moleen would sit watch last. Fargo saw the man—but he was lying on his side. Evidently he hadn't been able to stay awake.

Fargo sat up. All was quiet. Rising, he stepped to the deputy to wake him. "Clifton?" the man's name was. Fargo shook his shoulder. "Wake up, you lunkhead."

The deputy didn't stir.

"Clifton?" Fargo shook harder and the limp form rolled onto its back. Fargo bent, and swore.

The man's eyes were wide and glazed. His throat had been slit from ear to ear with so much force, it was a wonder the head was still attached.

Palming the Colt, Fargo turned. The quiet took on ominous meaning. He went to Moleen and the other deputy. The marshal's chest was rising and falling and the deputy was snoring. He nudged Moleen with his boot, hard, and the lawman's eyes snapped open.

"Fargo?"

"Your other deputy is dead," Fargo related. "Throat cut."

Just like that, Moleen was on his feet with his revolver out. "Comanches?" he whispered.

"Why only him and not the rest of us?" Fargo nodded at the string. "And the horses are still here." To the Comanches, good horses were as valuable as gold.

"Oster then?"

"Again, why only your deputy?" To Fargo's way of thinking, if Oster wanted anyone dead, it was him. Or was it? "Hell," he said, and ran to where Lacey Mayhare had been tied.

The lawman came with him. "She's gone!"

Fargo looked at the string again and this time he counted them. "Damn. I didn't notice. So are two of the horses."

"Why would Oster take her?"

Fargo looked at him.

"Oh," Moleen said. "We should wake up the others."

Fargo didn't see any need for it. Oster was gone, and there was nothing they could do until daylight.

Moleen disagreed. "He might deal with her and come back for the senator or someone else."

To say no one was particularly upset by Lacey's disappearance was an understatement.

"Serves her right, the way she behaved," Benton declared.

"She brought it on herself by shooting my wife," Senator Deerforth said.

Vin Creed raised his flask. "To the sweet and adorable Miss Mayhare. May she rest in peace."

"That's not funny," Marshal Moleen said.

Fargo was growing tired of the whole bunch. If not for Roselyn, he'd be long gone. He tried to get back to sleep but he didn't drift off until a few hours before dawn. He was up before sunrise and had the Ovaro saddled and ready.

Moleen was up too, drinking coffee by the fire. "One of us should go with you," he said, with a nod at his remaining deputy.

"You need to protect them," Fargo said, motioning at the others.

"We'll be heading back as soon as the sun is up. Catch up when you can."

Fargo found where Garvin Oster had led two horses from the far end of string. Oster had gone only about fifty yards to where his horse, and presumably Roselyn, bound and gagged, were waiting. Fargo figured that Oster had put Roselyn on one horse, thrown Lacey over the other, and climbed on the last animal. Their tracks pointed south.

For half an hour Fargo pushed at a trot. He wanted to

overtake them quickly but it wasn't to be. Oster had been pushing, too.

He reined up when he saw buzzards. How they gathered so quickly was a mystery. He counted six, circling with outspread pinions.

Clucking to the Ovaro, Fargo covered another half a mile.

He suspected what he would find—Lacey Mayhare, dead. He didn't foresee how grisly it would be.

Garvin Oster didn't simply shoot her. He cut off her fingers. He cut off her ears. He cut off her nose and stuffed it into her mouth. He cut open her belly, too, from hip bone to hip bone, and her innards had oozed out. The stink of the blood and her stomach juices was abominable. The buzzards hadn't been at her yet and her eyes were open and mirrored the horror that seized her at the end.

Fargo dug a shallow grave. He owed her that much. As he wiped his hands on his pants he said by way of a eulogy, "You were good in bed."

The tracks continued to the south—in the direction of town. Fargo kept expecting Oster to bear to the east or the west but after a while he realized that, as incredible as it seemed, Garvin Oster was going back. It made no sense, unless Oster wasn't satisfied with killing just Lacey.

Fargo pressed on. He was startled when he spied more buzzards. A jab of his spurs brought the Ovaro to a gallop and he swept over a low rise to behold another body lying off in the grass.

It was Roselyn.

45

Fargo was out of the saddle before the Ovaro came to a stop. He ran to her and knelt. "Damn it to hell."

The girl was belly down, her arms out-flung, blood trickling from a bullet wound to her head.

Certain he wouldn't find a pulse, Fargo pressed a finger to her wrist. He nearly whooped when he felt the beat of her heart. He carefully rolled her over. The wound he had taken for a bullet had been inflicted by a blunt object. A gun butt, possibly. He got his canteen, took off his bandanna, and moistened it. Gingerly, he dabbed at the blood.

Roselyn groaned.

Fargo sat and cradled her in his lap and went on cleaning the wound. It was another minute before her eyelids fluttered and opened.

"Skye?"

"Hush. I'm doctoring you."

"He hit me."

"No fooling."

Roselyn started to reach up.

"Lie still. It's not too deep. Your head will hurt for a few days and then you should be good as new."

"He hit me," Roselyn said again, "and left me for dead. After what he did to that poor woman—" She stopped and shuddered. "I begged him to stop. I pleaded with him to leave her be but he went on carving, and grinning."

"Grinning?"

"He's not in his right mind. You should have seen him when my mother was shot. He took me off a ways and made me sit while he paced and talked to himself. It was as if he'd gone mad. Every other word was a swear word, and he kept growling and hissing like an animal." Roselyn closed her eyes and smiled. "That feels nice, what you're doing."

"How did you end up here?"

Roselyn shuddered some more. "After what he did to Miss Mayhare, he took off my gag and asked me how did I like what he had done?" She looked up at him. "Why would he ask such a thing?"

"Go on," Fargo said.

"I told him he was terrible, that even if he is my father, I wanted nothing more to do with him. We argued, and everything I said made him madder and madder until he drew the six-gun he took from that deputy, and hit me."

"You were lucky."

Roselyn touched her head. "You call *this* luck?"

"He could have shot you or cut you up."

"No, I don't think he would go that far. He doesn't love me in the way my real father"—Roselyn caught herself—"He doesn't love me in the way the man I thought was my father does, but he does feel a certain fondness because he sired me."

"Where did he get to?"

"He didn't say where he was going. Frankly, I hope he disappears and we never see him again."

Fargo stepped to the Ovaro. After undoing his bedroll, he slid the Arkansas toothpick out and cut a strip from his blanket to use as a bandage. He applied it despite her protests that she didn't need one. "There. Now there's less chance of infection."

Roselyn raised adoring eyes. "I'm awful grateful for all you've done."

"I'd do it for anyone," Fargo said, which wasn't entirely true. He tied on the bedroll, climbed up, and offered his hand. Once she was behind him with her arms around his waist, he reined around and tapped his spurs.

"We're not heading for town?"

"The posse," Fargo said. "The senator is beside himself with worry."

"Is he sad over my mother?"

"What do you think?"

"To be honest, I don't know what to think anymore. My life has been turned upside down. A lot of what I took as true, isn't. I never would have imagined my mother having an affair with any man, let alone Garvin Oster."

"Makes two of us," Fargo said.

"Did she really love Oster or was it just . . . the other?"

"Sex?"

"I wish you wouldn't say that word."

"We'll call it the other, then," Fargo said, grinning. "It's all some people think about. As for your mother, I can't say."

"Is it all you think about?"

"Talk about something else."

"But I never get to talk about it, and I'm curious. My parents always acted embarrassed if I so much as mentioned kissing a boy."

"You'll find out about it yourself soon enough."

"Is it as good as they say?"

"Some folks like it."

"How about you?"

Fargo shrugged. "I can go without if I have to." Which was about the biggest lie he'd ever told.

"But it feels nice, doesn't it?"

"Some," Fargo said.

"You're not being much help. I'm trying to figure out why my mother was so attached to Garvin Oster."

"It could be she cared for him and liked doing the other, both," Fargo said.

Roselyn was quiet a while. Finally she said, "These have been the worst days of my life. What do we do when life kicks us in the teeth like this?"

"Kick back," Fargo said.

46

The reunion was touching. Senator Deerforth held her and cried and she sobbed into his chest.

Everyone else stood around looking uncomfortable.

Fargo walked off a short way and squatted and plucked at the grass. A shadow fell across him and a silver flask was dangled in front of his face.

"Care for a sip?" Vin Creed asked.

"Don't mind if I do." Fargo swallowed and savored the warmth that spread through his gut. He passed the flask back. "I'm obliged."

"Where do you reckon Oster got to?"

"No telling."

"If he's smart he'll hightail it clear out of Texas. Only he hasn't ever struck me as having a whole lot of brains."

"He had enough to run the senator's estate."

"And bed his wife." Creed sipped and let out a sigh. "I had my heart set on that one hundred thousand."

"There's always next year."

"No, there's not," Creed said. "While you were gone the senator mentioned that this was the last of his poker tournaments. He couldn't go through another. It would bring back painful memories." He gazed across the prairie. "It's just as well, I suppose. Texas is too rough and wild for my blood. I like New Orleans. It's more refined, more elegant."

"Elegant?" Fargo said, and laughed.

"Mock me if you will but I'm fond of my creature comforts." Creed held out the flask again and Fargo shook his head. "Yes sir. As soon as we get back, I'm packing and heading for a more civilized part of the country."

"I like the wild parts, myself."

"That's because in some ways you're more Injun than white. You don't mind spending days in the saddle. You like to sleep under the stars. You shoot and cook your own food." Creed shook his head. "Me, I'm fond of a soft bed and the best restaurants. And as for riding, my ass is so sore, it won't bother me a lick if I never sit a horse again."

Fargo chuckled.

A slug smashed into Creed's face a full second before the distant boom of the rifle, the force slamming him off his feet.

He was dead before he hit the ground.

Fargo dived flat and clawed at his Colt. He'd forgotten about Oster's Sharps. He twisted to yell at the others to do as he had done just as a second shot smashed into the deputy's chest and flipped him backward. "Get down!"

Marshal Moleen threw himself at Senator Deerforth and Roselyn and bore them to the earth with him, shielding them with his body.

The banker, Benton, gaped at the body of the deputy, his mouth opening and closing.

"Get down, you jackass!" Fargo hollered.

Benton looked up in bewilderment. "Where—?" he said. Instead of dropping flat he bent at the knees and reached down to lower himself. There was a *splat* and the top of his head blew off in a spectacular shower of skin and bone and what little hair he had. He fell like a dropped rock, his brains oozing from the hole.

"The rest of you stay down," Fargo said. "He can't see us in this grass."

Lead whistled overhead and a horse whinnied stridently. The blast came an instant later.

Fargo spun. The animal that belonged to Benton was staggering, blood pumping from its neck. Uttering another whinny, it keeled onto its side and kicked.

"He's going to kill the horses!" Moleen shouted.

Again lead scorched the air and the right eye of Creed's horse erupted in a spray of gore. The horse collapsed as if its legs were made of wax.

Pushing up, Fargo ran for the Ovaro. "We have to get out of here!" He veered to help the lawman pull the senator and the girl to their feet. Keeping hold of Roselyn, he flew to a sorrel and heaved her onto the saddle. "Head north!" he yelled, and smacked the animal on the rump. Whirling, he darted to the Ovaro. As his boot hooked the stirrup, a leaden messenger of death sizzled inches from his ear. Swinging up, he hauled on the reins.

Marshal Moleen was riding hell-bent for leather. Deerforth was slapping his legs and staring back in terror.

The other horses were scattering, including the one that bore Ginny's blanket-wrapped body.

Fargo dreaded that the next shot would bring the Ovaro down. He lashed the reins, anxious to get out of range. For more than half a mile he flew as if the dogs of hell were nipping at the stallion's hooves.

Ahead of him, the others seemed to ride into the very earth.

Momentarily, Fargo saw why: a basin covered half an acre. He galloped into it and came to a sliding stop.

"Damn that son of a bitch!" Marshal Moleen fumed. "Picking us off like that."

"He shot the poor horses too," Roselyn said. She was pale and wide-eyed.

Deerforth put a hand to his face and wiped at a smear of blood and something about the size of a silver dollar that clung to his cheek. He held it out. "Oh, God. I think this is part of Benton's head." He threw it down and wiped his fingers on his jacket.

"What do we do?" Roselyn asked, tears in her eyes. "If we show ourselves, he'll shoot more of us, won't he?"

"He sure as hell will," Fargo said.

47

The rest of the day crawled on claws of tension.

They decided to wait until nightfall. Fargo passed around jerky from his saddlebags and after they ate, Roselyn curled into a ball and fell into a fitful asleep. Moleen went to the basin rim to keep watch.

Senator Deerforth walked in small circles, wringing his hands. He was a man on the brink. Now and then he glanced at Fargo as if he were about to say something but didn't. Finally he came out with, "I have a favor to ask of you."

"After we get you and your girl back safe, I'll go look for your wife's body."

"No, it's not that." Deerforth hesitated. "I'd like for you to kill Garvin Oster."

Fargo stared. "I'm not an assassin."

"I know that. You're a scout, not a gun hand. You don't kill people for money. But you've killed before, and rumor has it you are good at it."

"I do what I have to to stay alive."

"Garvin has destroyed my life. He slept with my wife. He kidnapped my sweet child. Now he's shot one of my best friends, Stanley Benton. If anyone deserves to die, it's him."

Fargo didn't respond.

"Then there are the good citizens who have voted me into office so many times," Deerforth said forlornly.

"How the hell do they figure in?"

"Politics are my life. It's all I've lived for. I doubt the voters will have much respect for a man who can't hold on to his wife."

Fargo shook his head in disgust.

"What? It's true. I'll be voted out in the next election. And then what will I have?"

"Roselyn."

"Well, yes, that goes without saying. But all the meaning will be gone from my life. I'll lose the thing I hold most dear."

"It wasn't Ginny?" Fargo said.

"Why would it be her? She never did like my running for office. All she did was complain. I was away from home too much. I left her alone too often. Silly things like that." Deerforth still walked in circles. "She accused me of loving power more than I loved her. I told her that was ridiculous but she said if I truly cared, I would spend more time at home."

"Did you ever think she might be lonely?"

"She had friends. A social life. She didn't need me there all the time."

Fargo stared at a him, a notion taking shape. "Did you go to bed with other women?"

Deerforth stopped pacing. "What kind of question is that?" he demanded.

"A simple one. Were you faithful to your wife?"

"It's none of your business."

"You weren't," Fargo said.

The senator came closer. He glanced at his daughter and said quietly, "The reputation you have, why should it surprise you? A man has needs. When he's away from hearth and home he must meet those needs some other way."

"All of this," Fargo said.

"All of what?"

"Ginny was right about you."

"You're saying I'm to blame for our predicament?"

"It's not all on her," Fargo said.

"I say it is."

Fargo had to get away from him. He climbed the slope and sank down next to Marshall Moleen. "Anything?"

The lawman had taken off his hat. "If Garvin is out there, he's well hid."

"It'll be dark in an hour."

"If I was Garvin Oster," Moleen said, "I wouldn't let us reach town. All he has to do is lie in wait between here and there."

"We circle to the east."

"Unless he second-guesses us." The lawman leaned on an elbow. "Or we can second-guess him. You take the girl and circle east. I'll take Marion and circle west. One of us is bound to make it."

"I don't know." Fargo didn't like the notion of splitting up. "What else can we do?"

"Draw him to us," Fargo proposed. "Make a fire with enough smoke he's bound to see it."

Moleen caught on right away. "And rig our blankets so it looks like we're under them?"

"Only we'll be off in the high grass."

"You're a tricky bastard," Moleen said, and smiled. "I like that." He started to slide down. "Let me talk to the senator."

Fargo rested his chin on his arm and scoured the prairie for movement. He doubted Garvin would be that careless, but you never knew. After a while he heard someone climbing up to join him and thought it was the marshal. "What did the senator say?"

"That I wanted to talk to you first," Deerforth answered, and sank beside him. "How confident are you that your plan will work?"

"It might," Fargo said, "and it might not."

Deerforth frowned. "My daughter's life is at stake, to say nothing of our own. I need more assurance than that."

"It's a roll of the dice. If he wants you dead bad enough, he'll fall for it."

"Why me?"

"It's you he must hate the most. I suspect he'll save you for last."

"You're just guessing."

"It's a good guess. He'll probably cut on you like he did Lacey Mayhare."

Deerforth blanched. "My daughter told me about her. But what makes you say that?"

"Think about it," Fargo said. "He could have shot any of us back there. He picked Creed and the deputy and Benton. Men he hardly knew."

"He's working his way to me?" Deerforth licked his lips. "But why? Out of spite over Ginny? I didn't shoot her, that foolish woman did."

"You were Ginny's husband."

Deerforth ran a hand over his hair. "I won't be safe, will I, until he's dead?"

"No."

"Even if we make it past him and reach town, my life will always be in danger, won't it?"

"It will."

"Then yes, let's try your idea of luring him in. Let's end this once and for all."

"One way or the other," Fargo said.

48

Stars speckled the night sky, broken here and there by islands of clouds.

Fargo lay a dozen feet from the southeast rim of the basin in waist-high grass. He had been there for hours. It was almost midnight and Garvin Oster hadn't shown.

From where he lay Fargo couldn't see Marshal Moleen, who was off a ways, or the senator and Roselyn, who were well hid at the north end of the basin, well out of possible harm.

The fire had long since gone out but before it died it gave off enough light and smoke that if Oster was anywhere near, he was bound to spot it.

So where the hell was he? Fargo wondered. All this trouble they had gone to, and Oster might be too smart for them. He went to shift his legs and froze. Over by the basin something moved. He sought to pierce the dark, to tell if it was an animal. The grass swayed—or did he imagine it?

Fargo pressed the Henry to his shoulder and slowly thumbed back the hammer. The click was so slight that he wasn't worried Oster would hear. He waited for a glimpse of his target. Then, for a split instant a large bulk appeared at the brink of the basin. It was there and it was gone, too swiftly for him to shoot.

Fargo bit off a choice cussword. Lowering the rifle, he crawled. He used his elbows and his knees and tried to rustle the grass as little as possible. He came to the edge and peered over. The basin was a bowl of ink. All he could see were the black silhouettes of the horses.

The horses. Fear filled him—fear for the Ovaro—and he crabbed down into the ink, moving faster than he should but he wouldn't ever let anything happen to the stallion if he could help it. He'd ridden it for years now, and it meant more to him than most people.

He was making more noise than he should but it couldn't be helped. A third of the way in, he saw a form rise to his left. He rolled as the night pealed to man-caused thunder and heard the thwack of the slug striking the ground. Prone on his side, he fired, jacked the lever, fired again. The second shot was a waste. The figure had already sunk from sight.

Fargo fed another cartridge into the chamber while scrambling into a crouch. Had he hit Oster? He wasn't sure.

Minutes passed, and he stayed where he was. To move might draw lead.

"Fargo!" Marshal Moleen called down from the rim. "Are you all right?"

Fargo didn't answer. It would tell Oster where he was. The lawman should have known better. Then he realized—now Oster knew where Moleen was. Taking a gamble, he replied, "Watch yourself! He's down here somewhere." As he shouted, he dived, and it was well he did. The Sharps shattered the night, and the whistle of heavy lead nearly claimed his life.

Oster was good, damn good.

Fargo lay still. More minutes elapsed. The basin stayed still. He was beginning to think he would be there all night when a commotion broke out at the rim. There were blows and curses and a grunt. Throwing caution aside, he rose and raced for the top. When the commotion abruptly stopped, so did he.

Crouching, he listened.

The silence was deafening.

Fargo didn't move. He dared not make the same mistake again. His ears pricked at a slight scrape, as of a body dragging along the ground. Someone was crawling toward him.

He centered the Henry on a patch of grass and guessed right—the grass parted. A dark object the size of a melon poked out and he curled his finger around the trigger.

"Fargo?"

Moleen's voice was strangled with pain. Wary as a cat Fargo went over. The lawman was slumped flat. His hat was missing and his vest was torn. Fargo put a hand on his shoulder.

"Moleen?"

"The son of a bitch stabbed me," the lawman said into the dirt, his words muffled.

"Here," Fargo said, and carefully rolled him over. Dark blotches marked the shirt under the sternum. "How bad?" he whispered.

"Bad," Moleen rasped.

"I can't tend you until I know where he is." Fargo scanned the rim.

"He's gone," Moleen said. "I think you hit him. He was moving strange when he jumped me and when he crawled off."

The lawman coughed and dark spots appeared at the corners of his mouth. "I shouldn't have yelled."

"Keep it down," Fargo said. "He might circle around."

Moleen groaned. His hand rose feebly to his shirt. "So this is how it will be."

"Save your breath. Maybe it's not as bad as you think."

"No. He got me good. His knife went in to the hilt. He was going for the heart." Moleen coughed harder and blood trickled down his chin.

"I can get you some water."

"Don't bother."

They were quiet save for the lawman's heavy breathing, which grew slower and slower.

"Never been so wrong about anyone as I was about him," Moleen broke the silence. "I thought he'd given up his old ways."

"A wolf can be tamed but it's still a wolf," Fargo said.

Moleen sucked in a long breath. "Don't let him get the senator and the girl."

"I'll protect them the best I can." Fargo didn't add that it might not be good enough.

Moleen raised his face to the heavens. "A pretty night for dying."

"You're not dead yet."

"Yes," Moleen said. "I am."

The breathing sounds stopped.

49

Fargo had to say their names several times before Marion Deerforth answered. He led the horses to the spot where they were hidden. "You can stand up."

The senator rose, Roselyn clinging to him in fear. "We heard shots. I didn't know if it was safe."

"We're lighting a shuck." Fargo handed over the reins to their mounts.

"What about Marshal Moleen?" Deerforth peered at the basin. "Is he staying to cover our backs?"

"He's gone."

"Gone where?" Roselyn asked.

"Heaven or hell or nowhere. Take your pick." Fargo gripped the saddle horn, the saddle creaking under him.

"Hold on," Senator Deerforth said. "It's just the three of us now?"

Fargo told them about the lawman's death. They were shocked, Deerforth more than his daughter.

"I knew Floyd a good many years. He was as honest as they come. Dependable, too." He went to climb on his animal. "Wait. Did you bury him?"

"We don't have the time."

"Damn it, man. We can't leave him for the vultures and the coyotes."

"Listen to me," Fargo said. "Oster is out there somewhere. He might be hurt but that won't stop him from finishing what he's started. We have to go, now, and put as many miles as we can behind us before daylight."

"Listen to him, Father," Roselyn said.

Deerforth smiled. "Thank you for calling me that. I was

afraid you would regard Garvin as your parent now that the truth has come out."

"He didn't raise me. You did."

Going to her horse, Deerforth held up his hand and Roselyn clasped it. "It means the world to me that you still care for me."

From across the basin came a thud.

"Get on," Fargo commanded.

With the senator on his right and Roselyn on his left, they spent the next several hours fleeing south across the starlit plain.

Fargo needed a brainstorm, a way of turning the tables, but he was fresh out of ideas. Oster was too canny to fall for the same ruse twice.

Toward morning he was on the lookout for a place to lie low. Endless flat met his gaze.

"Skye," Roselyn spoke for the first time since midnight. "I can't keep my eyes open."

"Me either," the senator was quick to say. "I demand you let us rest. It's inhuman to push us so hard."

"Would you rather be dead?"

A swath of churned ground gave Fargo hope. A herd of buffalo had passed that way in the past few days, and where there were buffs, there were wallows. Wallows reeked of urine and in the heat of the day swarmed with flies but they were large enough and deep enough to conceal a horse and rider.

An arch of fire had risen to the east when Fargo found what he was looking for—half a dozen wallows. Drawing rein, he announced, "This is as far as we go."

"Thank God," Deerforth said.

Roselyn had to be helped off her horse. When Fargo started to usher her into a wallow she stopped and sniffed and scrunched up her face.

"You can't be serious."

"We'll rest and head out at sunset."

"Spend all day in *that*?" Roselyn shook her head. "I can't. It reeks to high heaven."

"It's just buffalo piss."

"Fargo, please," Senator Deerforth broke in. He hadn't climbed down yet. "Your language."

"I absolutely refuse," Roselyn said.

"You'll be safe."

"I'll be sick."

"If she doesn't want to, we can't make her," the senator declared.

"There's nowhere else," Fargo said impatiently. "We can't stay in the open."

"Surely we've lost him," Deerforth said. "We must have covered ten to twelve miles or better."

"It's not enough."

"He couldn't track us in the dark," Deerforth argued. "It will take him most of the day to overtake us, if he even can. I say we stop, yes. But I absolutely refuse to have you force my daughter into one of those awful wallows."

"Thank you," Roselyn said gratefully.

Deerforth smiled. "You've been through enough, my dear. Spread your blankets and get some sleep. I assure you we're quite safe."

That was when his face exploded.

50

For a split instant Fargo was riveted in disbelief. He shouldn't have been, not after Oster had already killed so many. Galvanizing to life, he seized Roselyn. She screamed and tried to pull free to run to her father but he threw her into the wallow.

Grabbing the reins to the Ovaro and to her horse, Fargo pulled them in after him. Hers balked. Suddenly it squealed and staggered; part of its head had been blown away.

Letting go of its reins, he hauled on the Ovaro's. He was deathly afraid the Sharps would thunder again and the stallion would share its fate.

A few bounds and they were in the wallow. Fargo started to go for the senator's animal but another shot brought it crashing down before he could reach it.

Fargo swore and shucked the Henry from the scabbard. Roselyn was in a crouch, her arms around her chest, bawling hysterically. He put a hand on her shoulder and gently squeezed.

"Get hold of yourself."

"He's dead!" Roselyn wailed, and swatted his hand off. "That terrible man killed him!"

Fargo tried to comfort her and was rebuffed. Leaving her to her grief, he went up the wallow and hunkered. Taking off his hat, he peered over. The shot horses were limp, red pools forming. Deerforth was on his back, what was left of his face oozing scarlet.

As the prairie brightened, Fargo searched in vain for some sign of Garvin Oster. He was about to sink back and ponder his options when a figure rose out of the grass to the north.

He couldn't believe his eyes. It had to be Oster—and he

was coming toward them. He snapped the Henry to his shoulder and waited for Oster to come in range.

It struck him that Oster seemed taller than he should be, and that there was something odd about the way the man was moving. Presently he saw why.

Oster was holding his hands over his head and walking with a shuffling gait, as if each step were a trial.

"What the hell?"

Fargo centered the Henry on Oster's chest. Soon Oster was in range but he didn't fire. On Oster came. Five hundred yards out, Oster stumbled. At two hundred yards, a crimson stain on Oster's shirt suggested why. At fifty yards Oster stopped and seemed to be having trouble breathing. He advanced, tottering. At twenty yards, his pasty face, slick with sweat, confirmed what Fargo already knew—Oster was a dead man walking.

Fargo rose out of the wallow, covering him. "That's far enough."

Garvin Oster came to a halt. He licked his lips and croaked, "I don't have long left."

"I can see that," Fargo said. "Marshal Moleen's doing?"

"Yours," Oster said, "when we swapped lead last night." He coughed violently. "You're a regular hellion."

"Lucky shot," Fargo said.

"I'd like—" Oster swayed and grunted and steadied himself. "I'd like to see her before I cash in."

"I doubt she wants to see you. You just killed her father, you stupid son of a bitch."

"*I'm* her pa," Oster exclaimed with a flash of vehemence. "Where is she? Call to her." He looked past Fargo. "Is that a wallow? Tell her I'm here. Leave it to her."

Fargo would just as soon shoot him. "Where's your Sharps and your six-gun?"

"I left them with my horse," Oster said. "You're welcome to all of it once I'm gone."

Fargo glanced over his shoulder. Roselyn was still sniffling and sobbing. "Roselyn?"

She didn't look up.

"Roselyn, he's here."

Slowly raising her head, Roselyn blinked and said, "Who is?"

"Who do you think?"

"Him?"

"He's hurt bad. He wants to see you before he dies."

Roselyn dabbed at her eyes, smearing dirt on her cheek. She stiffly rose and timidly approached, stopping when she set eyes on the man who had sired her.

Garvin Oster smiled. "I wanted to see you one last time, girl. I wanted to tell you how sorry I was."

"Sorry?" Roselyn said, and uttered a peculiar little high-pitched laugh.

"I'm sorry things didn't work out," Oster said. "Your ma was lookin' forward to us bein' together. It was important to her, not livin' a lie anymore."

Her face twisting in anger, Roselyn came out of the wallow. "What about what was important to me?"

"She loved you, girl," Oster said.

"I don't love her. Not anymore. Not after what she put me through."

"You don't mean that. She was tryin' to set things right. You can't hold that against her."

Roselyn's face began twitching. She laughed again, a laugh so strange and piercing, it brought a look of confusion to Garvin Oster.

"What in the world is the matter with you?"

Roselyn went on laughing and twitching. Suddenly she whirled, snatched Fargo's Colt from his holster, and ran at Oster. Fargo tried to grab her but she was too quick. The next moment she jammed the Colt's muzzle against Oster's mouth, nearly knocking him down. "Fuck you!" she screamed, and shot him. The back of Oster's head exploded and he rocked onto his boot heels, his eyes wide in amazement.

Fargo started to reach for her but lowered his arm.

Roselyn was crying and laughing at the same time. "What's the matter with me?" she screeched. "I'll show you what's the matter with me." She shot Oster in the chest. His legs buckled and he fell to his knees. "You're what's the matter with me," she shrieked, and shot him in the groin. "You, you, you," she cried, and with each "you", the Colt blasted anew. She thumbed the hammer and squeezed the trigger once more; there was a click. She went on thumbing and squeezing: click, click, click, click.

Fargo came around and took the Colt. She didn't resist. She stood staring at the bulk at their feet.

"I killed him."

"You sure as hell did."

"I didn't mean to."

"You sure as hell did," Fargo said again.

Roselyn sniffled and said, "Yes, I suppose I did. And do you know what? It felt good."

"Careful, girl," Fargo said, smiling, "or you'll turn out like me."

"Oh, God," Roselyn said.

LOOKING FORWARD!
The following is the opening
section of the next novel in the exciting
***Trailsman* series from Signet:**

TRAILSMAN #361
UTAH DEADLY DOUBLE

Utah Territory, 1859—
where a ruthless master of disguise turns
Fargo into the most wanted man in the West.

"Gentlemen," announced the young drummer from Pennsylvania, "there seems to be something a mite queer about this game."

An ominous silence followed his remark. The other four poker players, including Skye Fargo, swiveled their heads to stare at him.

"No offense intended," the salesman hastened to add.

"Well, plenty taken, you mouthy jackanapes," growled Billy Williams, who was assisting Fargo on a scouting mission for the much-ballyhooed Pony Express, due to be launched next year. He scowled darkly and scraped his chair back to clear his gun hand.

"H'ar now!" cautioned Red Robinson from behind the crude plank bar. The burly, redheaded Irishman owned the only saloon—actually just a primitive grog shop—permitted at Fort Bridger by the Mormon Council in Salt Lake City. "Stay your hand, Old Billy. This ain't Laredo. These soldiers in the Mormon Battalion are no boys to mess with. The last gentile who cracked a cap in this pukehole spent three months in the stockade."

"Come down off your hind legs, Old Billy," Fargo threw in, strong white teeth flashing through his neatly cropped beard as he grinned. "Mr. Brubaker here didn't accuse any of us. He simply pointed out there's something a mite queer about the game."

"That's what the lawyers call tantamount to an accusation," chimed in Lemuel Atkins, a Mormon doctor at Fort Bridger who often violated the social order to indulge his love of pasteboard thrills with gentiles, the Mormon word for anyone outside their religion.

"Tanny mount, my hinder," the hotheaded Billy fumed. "Let's kill the young pup with a knife, then, and go snooks on his money. He's called all of us cheaters, ain't he?"

"Not quite," said the fifth player at the table, Sy Munro, an outfitter for pilgrims passing through Fort Bridger on their way to the Sierra gold fields and coast settlements. He wore new range clothes and a clean neckerchief. "I'd say he just implied it."

"Imply a cat's tail!" protested Old Billy. "You heard the doc—it was tanny mount! The snivelin' little scrote called every last one of us cheaters."

"If he did," put in Fargo calmly, shifting a skinny Mexican cigar to the other side of his mouth, "he spoke straight-arrow. Matter fact, he's the only one at the table who *ain't* cheating. It's him ought to shoot us."

Every jaw at the table dropped, including Lonny Brubaker's.

"Fargo," warned Old Billy, "you *had* teeth when you got here."

Fargo ignored his blustering partner, looking at the dumbfounded drummer. "Mr. Brubaker, have you ever heard of the cheater's table?"

"The . . . no, sir."

"It's a custom that started on the Mississippi riverboats. When trade is slow for the professional gamblers, they get up a game among themselves to hone their cheating skills."

"You mean I just happened along when one of those games was going on here?"

"We're not professionals," Fargo conceded, "but we figured to have a little fun. Old Billy has been crimping cards, Sy smudging them with his cigar, and Doc Atkins has been dealing from every place *except* the top of the deck."

"How 'bout you?"

Fargo grinned. "Every time the doc blew cigar smoke in your face, you turned in my direction and showed me your cards—which ain't cheating, by the way. Learn to cover your cards, son."

Brubaker's smooth-shaven face looked astounded. "Well, I'm clemmed!"

"How much did you drop tonight?" Fargo added.

"Well, twelve dollars."

Fargo counted out three silver dollars from his pile and slid them to Brubaker. "C'mon, boys," he called to the others. "Time to post the pony."

Old Billy loosed a string of epithets worthy of a stable sergeant. Fargo's partner on this Pony Express assignment was a homely cuss with a twice-broken nose and a large birthmark coloring the left side of his face reddish-purple. He was still in his thirties but had earned the moniker Old Billy because of his full mane of white-streaked hair—a legacy of nearly twenty years spent fighting some of the most bellicose tribes of the Southwest and Far West. His widespread reputation as an Indian fighter convinced Fargo to get him on the payroll.

"Fargo," he said in a tone heavy with disgust, "the hell's got into you—religion?"

"No, Fargo's right," Doc Atkins said as he counted out three dollars. "I never intended to keep the lad's money. Besides, though it's my own people, Red is correct—scratch a Mormon and you'll find a jailer. Best to take the peace road."

"I don't give a damn what you weak sisters do," Old Billy said stubbornly. "A man shouldn't step in something he can't wipe off, and that's what this clabber-lipped greenhorn done. What's next? We powder his butt and tuck him in? I ain't paying back one red cent."

Fargo watched Old Billy with speculative eyes. "Yeah, I've noticed something peculiar about you. You won't spend money except to gamble and make more. Won't even pony up a dime for a beer. I've never seen a bachelor behave like that."

Old Billy averted his eyes. "So I'm a damn miser. No law agin it."

Fargo shook his head and counted another three dollars out of his own money. "Satan won't allow you into hell, Old Billy—afraid you'll take over."

During this exchange no one had noticed when the cowhide flap that served as a door was suddenly thrust aside. The woman who stepped inside the smoky, dimly lit hovel had a pretty face that was creased from worry and suffering— a familiar sight on the frontier. No one noticed her in the murky shadows until the loud click of a mule-ear hammer being thumbed back seized their attention.

Suddenly all eyes were riveted on the steel-eyed woman with a German fowling piece in her hands. No great threat at a distance, up close like this it could shred a man's face—or his sex gear, Fargo thought, noticing she was aiming it right at him and below the belt. Sweat trickled out of his hairline.

"Why, Dot," Lemuel Atkins said, "what in the—?"

"Put a stopper on your gob, Doc," she snapped, never taking her fiery eyes off Fargo. "You with the buckskins and beard—is that your black-and-white pinto tethered outside?"

"It is, ma'am."

"And be your name Fargo?"

The Trailsman nodded, not liking the determined set of her face nor the dangerous turn this trail was taking.

"Then I'm here to kill you, mister."

Old Billy snickered. "See? Like I warned you, Fargo, never tell 'em you'll be right back. Some believe you."

The woman swung the muzzle toward Old Billy. "Shut your filthy sewer, you prairie rat. This is an over-and-under gun, and both barrels shoot. All of you keep that in mind before you play the hero."

"Hero?" Old Billy repeated. "Lady, it's none of my mix. Fargo stepped into this and he can wipe it off."

"Ma'am, I don't even know you," Fargo said, his voice calmer than he felt.

Lemuel spoke up quickly. "Skye Fargo, this is Dorothy Kreeger. Her husband died of snakebite a hundred miles west of South Pass on their way to settle in San Francisco. She has a seventeen-year-old daughter, Ginny, and—"

"Oh, this randy stallion knows Ginny, all right," Dot cut in. "In fact, he raped her not two hours ago in the hay fields just south of here. And then he beat her bloody and sliced up her limbs with that vicious knife in his boot."

Dead silence followed her remark. All eyes turned to Fargo. On the frontier a woman's accusation carried more force than a man's.

"Ma'am," Fargo said, "I don't call women liars, but I do call them mistaken. I'm sorry about your daughter, but I didn't have thing one to do with it. I've not met the lady."

"I'd hardly expect you to sign a confession. That's why I'm going to shoot you. You men sitting close to Fargo—spread out. I've no call to shoot anyone but him."

Red Robinson spoke up. "Dot, you're mighty mistaken. Two hours ago, you say? Couldn't a been Fargo—he's been right here playing poker for the past four hours."

"That's right," Doc Atkins chipped in. "Besides, I've known Fargo for years. He's the last man to commit a crime like that."

"Oh, I'd expect all of you to take his part. He's the famous Trailsman and all men look up to him. You men are pack animals—what's my girl compared to the high-and-mighty Trailsman?"

"Dot, you got that bass ackwards," Sy cut in. "This is the West. Why, President Buchanan himself would be drag-hanged for treating a female that way."

"Lady," spoke up Billy, barely suppressing a smirk, "Skye Fargo is a skunk-bit coyote, all right. Rotten as they come. I'd shoot the son of a buck."

"Heathens and Mormons," she said with bitter contempt. "Thinking this is all a big joke for your pleasure. My girl described her attacker, and this tall galoot fits the description right down to the ground. You, the young fellow closest to Fargo—get clear, I said, or you'll get the balance of these pellets."

Fargo could see that Lonny Brubaker was so scared he'd turned fish-belly white. But he stubbornly shook his head.

"No, ma'am. Mr. Fargo is innocent. He was right here when you say your daughter was accosted."

"Scootch over, Lonny," Fargo said in a take-charge voice. "If Mrs. Kreeger is bound and determined to cut me down in cold blood, no use you getting plugged, too."

"Hold off, Dot," Doc Atkins implored. "Take a good, long look at Fargo. Does he really look like the kind of man who'd need to . . . ravish a woman?"

Dorothy did look at Fargo, long and hard. For the first time, a look of uncertainty crossed her features. "He's mighty rugged and handsome," she admitted. "Well knit, too. I 'spect women flock to him like flies to sugar."

Old Billy didn't like the turn this trail was taking. "Sure, lady, but you know, some men prefer to make it rough with a woman—gets 'em more het up. I'd shoot him."

"I 'spect a man as ugly as you *has* to be rough," she replied. "Only way you can get it."

She looked speculatively at Fargo. "It's no secret that my Ginny likes men. I've heard all the jokes about how she's 'second-hand' and her sheets are always wrinkled. And the Lord knows there's precious few males at Fort Bridger to catch a young girl's eye. A man like you wouldn't have to attack her—unless he was sick in the brain."

"I don't dally with girls," Fargo told her. "Only women. Mrs. Kreeger, I don't doubt Ginny's word. But I'm not the only man on the frontier who wears buckskins. And the black-and-white pinto is no rare horse."

"No, but it is rare to see a white man riding a stallion. Mostly it's only Indians who don't cut their horses."

Fargo nodded. "I can't gainsay that."

"Can you gainsay that Arkansas toothpick in your boot or that brass-frame rifle in your saddle scabbard? What about the close-cropped beard and your black plainsman's hat? Ginny described all of it."

Fargo shrugged helplessly. "All I can tell you, ma'am, is that I'm innocent. Shouldn't we at least go talk to your daughter before you shoot me?"

She considered this for a few moments, and Fargo thought she was wavering. Then her face set itself hard and she shook her head no.

Her finger slipped inside the trigger guard and curled around the trigger. "No," she said, her voice implacable. "I'm going to kill you now before I go weak-kneed."

No other series packs this much heat!

THE TRAILSMAN

**Follow the trail of Penguin's Action Westerns at
penguin.com/actionwesterns**